P9-DOC-000

He wasn't what she expected.

For a bachelor who'd grown up with brothers, Liam had endless patience with her two little girls who chattered nonstop on the canoe ride. And now he was surprising her again.

"What's that?" she asked him as he approached her with a white box.

"Happy birthday, Anna." He opened it and took out a cake with one candle.

She couldn't stop her smile. "I can't remember the last time I had a birthday cake."

She reached for the knife, but the girls stopped her. "You have to blow out your candle first, Mom!"

Liam lit the candle. "Make a wish," he murmured.

Inexplicably, tears stung her eyes as she struggled to think of something. She closed them.

I wish...I wish I still believed wishes came true.

She blew out the candle and opened her eyes. Liam stood there huddled over the cake with her two little girls at his side, and she couldn't help her next thought.

Maybe her wish had already come true.

USA TODAY bestselling author **Kathryn Springer** grew up in a small town in northern Wisconsin, where her parents published a weekly newspaper. As a child, she spent many hours at her mother's typewriter, plunking out stories that her older brother "published" (he had the stapler!) for a nominal fee. When Kathryn isn't at the computer, she enjoys reading other people's books and spending time with her family and friends.

The Bachelor's Twins

Kathryn Springer

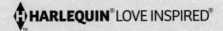

If you purchased this book without a cover you should be aware that this book is stolen property. It was reported as "unsold and destroyed" to the publisher, and neither the author nor the publisher has received any payment for this "stripped book."

Recycling programs
for this product may
not exist in your area.

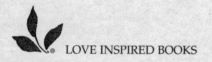 LOVE INSPIRED BOOKS

ISBN-13: 978-0-373-89928-9

The Bachelor's Twins

Copyright © 2017 by Kathryn Springer

All rights reserved. Except for use in any review, the reproduction or utilization of this work in whole or in part in any form by any electronic, mechanical or other means, now known or hereinafter invented, including xerography, photocopying and recording, or in any information storage or retrieval system, is forbidden without the written permission of the editorial office, Love Inspired Books, 195 Broadway, New York, NY 10007 U.S.A.

This is a work of fiction. Names, characters, places and incidents are either the product of the author's imagination or are used fictitiously, and any resemblance to actual persons, living or dead, business establishments, events or locales is entirely coincidental.

This edition published by arrangement with Love Inspired Books.

® and TM are trademarks of Love Inspired Books, used under license. Trademarks indicated with ® are registered in the United States Patent and Trademark Office, the Canadian Intellectual Property Office and in other countries.

www.Harlequin.com

Printed in U.S.A.

Carry each other's burdens, and in this way
you will fulfill the law of Christ.
—*Galatians* 6:2

To Stacey Orr, librarian extraordinaire,
who somehow knows the promise of coffee
and chocolate will get an introverted writer
to leave her office! But more than that, your
gracious hospitality makes public speaking
(something that ordinarily strikes fear in the heart
of said introverted writer!) feel more like
spending an afternoon with friends.
Thank you for bringing books and people together!

Chapter One

"Hold still, Liam! Remember, this is for a good cause."

Liam Kane smothered a sigh while his mom fussed with the silk square sprouting from the pocket of his vest.

"I'm holding."

Even though it was the third time she'd fussed with it.

Even though the needle on the outdoor thermometer was inching toward seventy-five degrees. A comfortable temperature for the middle of June in Michigan's Upper Peninsula—unless, of course, you happened to be wearing a tuxedo. Then, not so much.

A bead of sweat trickled down the side of Liam's face, only to be absorbed by the lime-green noose—okay, technically it was a *bow tie*—clipped to the front of his shirt. "Tell me again why Aiden isn't the one wearing this getup?"

Everyone knew Liam's fun-loving, extroverted kid brother never minded being the center of attention. Tourist or local, whenever someone booked a day trip with Castle Falls Outfitters, they invariably requested Aiden to be their guide. Not that Liam cared. He preferred to spend his days in the shop, designing and building canoes for the family business instead of paddling them down the river.

"He was supposed to." Liam's adoptive mom—"Sunni" to her friends and family because the nickname fit her warm, cheerful personality—plucked a loose thread dangling from one of the buttons on his shirt. "But the director of the Timber Shores Retreat Center called this morning in a bit of a panic, wondering if someone could give her new counselors some guiding tips. Aiden volunteered."

"How—" convenient...*clever?* "—nice of him."

"I thought so, too." Sunni took a step back and studied the finished product, smiling her approval before she turned to the newest member of the Kane family. "What do you think, Lily?"

Liam's sister-in-law, who'd been watching the transformation take place from her perch on the window seat, tried to hide her amusement. And the camera Liam had seen her aim in his direction. "I think Liam looks very, um…dashing."

Both women giggled, and Liam shook his head. There was no use confiscating the camera, though. In less than an hour he would be on display for the whole town to see, doing his part to raise funds for the animal shelter's new addition. Population-wise, Castle Falls didn't so much as warrant a dot on the map. But winters were long and the rest of the seasons notoriously short, so people would probably turn out in droves for the first community-wide event of the summer.

Liam suspected the timing was part of Sunni's plan.

"What's so funny—" Brendan, Liam's older brother, sauntered into the room, took one look at him and laughed. "Never mind."

Relief shot through Liam. "I thought you had a meeting this morning."

"Postponed until next week." Brendan hooked one arm around Lily's trim waist and tucked her against his side. "I'm free for the rest of the day."

"Great." Liam sent up a silent but heartfelt prayer of thanks. "You can take my place at the fund-raiser."

"I'm sure Lily could use Brendan's help overseeing the children's area." Sunni smiled at the newlyweds. "Besides that, I don't think there's time for you to change, sweetheart. And speaking of time…" She glanced at the clock above Brendan's desk. "The Sunflowers volunteered to handle the bake sale, and I promised Anna I would unlock the shelter a few minutes early so she and Rene Shapiro can help the girls set up."

Liam knew only one Anna who had children in the Wednesday night kids' club at church.

The bow tie around his neck suddenly felt even tighter.

"Oh, don't look so *hangdog*, bro." Brendan clapped a hand on Liam's shoulder.

"I've got two words for you," Liam growled. "Dunk tank."

Sunni cast a worried look in his direction even as Brendan struggled to keep a straight face.

"It's okay, Mom. I'm sure Liam's bark is worse than his bite."

Liam rolled his eyes. "Are you finished?"

Brendan pondered the question for a moment. Grinned. "Probably not."

Fine. Liam could take it. He would do just about anything for Sunni Mason, the woman who, had opened her home to three aspiring juvenile delinquents and raised them as her own.

He'd shake people's hands. Pass out brochures. *And* stay out of Anna Leighton's way—something he'd gotten pretty good at since she'd returned to Castle Falls six years ago, a grieving young widow with two-year-old twins in tow.

Fortunately for him, the last one would be a little easier since he'd be dressed up as the animal shelter's official goodwill ambassador, Dash the Dalmatian.

"I hope we have a turnout this good for our class reunion, Anna."

"So do I." Anna Leighton tucked a loaf of apple-rhubarb bread into a paper sack and smiled at Heather Cohen, a former classmate who'd finally worked her way to the front of the line at the bake-sale table. "Maybe we should have asked Sunni Mason to head up the planning committee for the reunion."

The promise of a beautiful summer day had drawn a large crowd, but Anna suspected that Sunni, the animal shelter's newly appointed president, was at least partially responsible for the excellent turnout.

Sunni had approached all the local business owners a few months prior to the fund-raiser and asked if they would be willing to donate an item or service for a silent auction. The winners wouldn't be announced until the end of the event, a brilliant plan that encouraged families to take advantage of a wide variety of activities and purchase something to eat from one of the many food booths.

So far, Anna had been too busy to see if anyone had bid on the necklace and bracelet she'd spent hours creating in her studio above The Happy Cow. The ice-cream shop paid the bills, but Anna dreamed of the day she could focus exclusively on *Anna's Inspiration*, the hand-crafted jewelry business that fed her soul.

Most of her sales were through word of mouth, but Anna had taken her friend Lily Kane's suggestion and left a stack of business cards next to the bid sheet in case someone wanted to place an order after the auction closed. Lily, who'd worked for the prestigious marketing firm Pinnacle before moving to Castle Falls, had shared a lot of great ideas to increase Anna's customer base.

Now if only she could find a few more hours in the day to implement them.

"Everyone knows you're going to do a fabulous job with our ten-year reunion." Heather finished counting out the change for her purchase and handed the money to Anna. "You never let us down when you were class president!

Heather drifted toward the silent auction table, and Anna made a mental note to check her email when she got home. With the reunion less than three weeks away, the number of RSVPs had continued to rise as the deadline on the invitation got closer.

"That's the last of the cinnamon rolls." Rene Shapiro, the Sunflowers' dedicated leader and a seasoned bake-sale veteran, pocketed a handful of change. "I'd send the girls on another kitchen run to restock our inventory, but I gave them all a five-minute break while Pastor Seth takes his turn in the dunk tank."

"I'll round them up," Anna offered. When it came to the lively group of third-grade girls—and her twins, in particular—five minutes could easily turn into ten. Or twenty.

She wove her way through the maze of picnic blankets spread out on the grass. Knowing Cassie and Chloe, they'd probably lost interest in the dunk tank and made their way over to the meet-and-greet tent again, where visitors could interact with some of the animals up for adoption.

Halfway there, her gaze snagged on two little sprites whose copper hair glowed almost as bright as the neon T-shirts the Sunflowers had tie-dyed at their last meeting. Only this time, the twins weren't cuddling puppies. They were talking to a six-foot-tall Dalmatian dressed in a tuxedo.

It had to feel like a sauna inside the furry suit and full-face mask, but "Dash," the animal shelter's mascot, had been circulating through the crowd all morning, greeting families and handing out pamphlets that included a miniature blueprint of the new addition.

A lively carnival tune began to blast through the speakers in a nearby booth. As Anna drew closer, she saw Cassie and Chloe each grab one of the Dalmatian's giant paws. Dash responded by breaking into a comical dance that looked like a cross between a waltz and a polka.

"Mom!"

Before Anna could react—or resist—Cassie grabbed her hand and swept her into the small circle of dancers. Her protest was drowned out by a burst of applause from the people standing near the booth.

Anna tipped her head back, trying to catch a glimpse of the man behind the mask, but dark mesh screens strategically placed in the mascot's oversize sunglasses concealed his identity.

Out of the corner of her eye, Anna saw Sunni Mason clapping with the beat of the music. The proud smile on her face was a good indication one of her sons had agreed to play the part.

By process of elimination, Anna concluded it had to be Aiden. Brendan was overseeing the children's area with Lily and Liam, and…well, it was common knowledge the most introverted of the three brothers tended to avoid social gatherings.

Just like he avoided her…

"It's your turn, Mom!"

In a synchronized choreography, Cassie and

Chloe nudged her closer to Dash, their giggles a melody that lightened Anna's heart even as the Dalmatian bowed and extended a furry paw.

For a moment, for her daughters, Anna set aside all the responsibilities crowding her mind—the stack of bills on the kitchen table and the daily pressures that came from trying to run two businesses and a busy household— and dropped a curtsy in response.

A split second later, she was in Dash's arms, waltzing across the grass.

Liam had heard the term *déjà vu*, but he'd never experienced it. Until now.

Because the moment Anna had stepped into his arms, Liam had taken a step back in time.

They'd danced together at their senior prom, too, although she'd been Anna Foster at the time. Head cheerleader. Class president. Honor-roll student.

Ross Leighton's steady girlfriend.

But that night, Liam hadn't cared. When he saw Ross grab Anna's arm in the parking lot, Liam had experienced an instant, gut-wrenching flashback from his own childhood. So while his classmates drank punch and flirted, Liam had waited for an opportunity to get alone so he could warn her about Ross.

And because Anna was Anna—beautiful and

polite—she'd accepted Liam's awkward invitation to dance. But as soon as the lights dimmed, he'd steered her through the open gymnasium doors into the courtyard instead.

Tiny lights had winked in the trees, mimicking the courtship of the fireflies, and swags of ivory netting woven around the posts of the rented gazebo had fluttered in the scented breeze.

Anna had looked up at him, surprise registering in her beautiful amber eyes, and Liam had almost lost his nerve.

If only he had.

Watching Anna's initial surprise change to confusion and then anger was a memory permanently etched in Liam's brain.

It must have become etched in Anna's, too, because ten years later, she still wouldn't look him in the eye.

But how could he blame her?

If Anna's vehement denial that Ross had mistreated her wasn't enough to convince Liam he'd been wrong, the grief shadowing Anna's eyes when she'd returned to Castle Falls confirmed it.

Ross may have had a personal ax to grind against Liam for being an "outsider," but he was also the town's beloved star quarterback. The guy who sat on the back of the mayor's vintage convertible and tossed Tootsie Rolls to the little kids at every parade. The guy with the perfect smile from the perfect family who'd swept Anna off her feet and carried her away into the perfect future.

The guy Liam had called abusive.

The crackle of a microphone drew everyone's attention to the makeshift stage that shelter volunteers had set up on the lawn and Anna smiled up at Liam as he released her.

"I should get back to the bake sale, Aiden." She caught her lower lip between her teeth. "Oops. I mean Dash. You have to maintain your cover, don't you?"

Liam sucked in a quiet breath behind his mask.

Apparently he did.

Because Anna assumed she'd been dancing with his *brother*.

Well, that explained a lot. Like Anna's whimsical little curtsy. Her willingness to step into his arms.

Her smile.

For a split second, when Anna had taken his hand, Liam thought that maybe she'd decided to put the past behind them. That maybe…just maybe…she'd forgiven him for crossing a line and, in the process, ruining what should have been one of the most special nights of her life.

Something Ross had taken issue with when he'd tracked Liam down after the dance and delivered a warning of his own—a warning accompanied by a few well-placed punches—to stay away from Anna in the future.

But Liam had had to live with the knowledge that he'd made a much more costly mistake than interfering in Anna's life that night.

By letting the shadow of the past cloud his perspective, he was the one who'd hurt her.

Chapter Two

"Please say you saved one of Mrs. Callahan's peanut butter fudge brownies for me."

Lily landed in front of the bake-sale table, a desperate look in her violet eyes.

"Sorry. I can't." Anna tried not to smile as she reached down and retrieved a foil-covered plate from the cooler near her feet. "Because I saved *two* for you."

"See? This is why we're friends." Lily released a contented sigh. "You know all my deepest, darkest secrets. My weakness for chocolate in any form. My hostility toward day planners."

If those were Lily's deepest, darkest secrets, she truly was a woman blessed.

"And don't forget your absolute devotion to your brilliant, good-looking husband." Brendan Kane came up behind Lily and looped his arm around her shoulders.

"There is that." Lily grinned up at her husband and the look that passed between them raised the temperature in the air a few more degrees.

Anna ignored a pinch of envy.

A few weeks ago she and the twins had watched the couple exchange vows in a beautiful ceremony on the riverbank near Sunni's home with all their friends and family in attendance. A ceremony so different from Anna's wedding day.

She and Ross had been married in front of a justice of the peace in a stuffy room devoid of decoration—unless a person counted the black-and-white portraits of dour-faced judges that lined the walls. Their only witnesses were a bailiff and the harried-looking secretary whose lunch they'd interrupted.

Anna shook away the memory.

It wasn't like Ross had kidnapped her and forced her into eloping with him. Anna had been so eager to start their life together that nothing else seemed to matter at the time. Not flowers or a fancy wedding gown or even whose names had been added to theirs on the marriage certificate after the judge pronounced them husband and wife.

"It's time to announce the winners of the silent auction!" Sunni had returned to the stage, waving a piece of paper in the air like a victory banner.

"Come on, Bren. Let's see if we won that Month of Sundaes from The Happy Cow." Lily winked at Anna as she grabbed her husband's hand and led him away.

Anna shook the crumbs from the tablecloth and folded it up as the microphone picked up Sunni's lilting voice and funneled it through the speakers.

"Our first item…a two-night stay at the bed-and-breakfast…goes to Pastor Seth Tamblin."

Rebecca Tamblin's shriek of delight was a clue she hadn't seen her husband bid on the romantic getaway.

Sunni waited for the applause to subside before she continued down the list. As she called out the names of the winners and the prizes they'd won, Anna was impressed at how many businesses had contributed something to the cause.

"Now, for our final item on the auction block today." If possible, Sunni's smile grew even wider. "A half-day guided canoe trip that includes sunshine, calm water, and a gourmet meal cooked over an open fire. And it goes to—" her gaze swept over the crowd, searching for the lucky winner "Anna Leighton! Come up and claim your prize!"

Her prize.

But…*how*?

Anna hadn't bid on anything.

The crowd had already started to disperse by the time she reached the stage.

"Sunni? Do you mind if I take a look at that bid sheet?"

"Of course not." The woman hopped down from the platform with the ease of someone half her age and handed Anna the piece of paper.

Sure enough, there was her name. In someone else's handwriting. Just as Anna had expected. A forgery.

"Is something wrong?" Sunni's brow knit with concern.

"I didn't bid on the canoe trip." Anna looked around for her daughters. Her adorable, precocious, exasperating daughters.

"But I'm pretty sure I know who did."

And they were skipping toward her, hand in hand, without an ounce of guilt weighing them down.

Anna held up the bid sheet. "Would you like to explain this, please?"

Two pairs of golden-brown eyes blinked up at her.

"We wanted it to be a surprise," Chloe said earnestly. "For your birthday."

"My birthday." Anna had been so busy finalizing details for her class reunion and keeping up with the steady stream of tourists flowing through Castle Falls as they made their way to the Lake Superior shoreline, she'd totally forgotten she had one coming up.

"Grandi told us she'd left some money in her dresser drawer and we should buy something special for you," Chloe explained. "And we're going to add the change in our piggy banks, too."

"We can earn our Sunflower Celebrate Creation pin and celebrate your birthday at the same time." Cassie grinned.

"Multitasking, right, Mom?"

Multi—

Anna was the one who felt a stab of guilt.

How many times over the past few months had the girls heard her use that particular word?

Anna struggled for balance, but it was challenging to keep things running smoothly at home and at work. Birthday or not, a leisurely day canoeing down the river seemed like an indulgence for a single working mom whose time would be better spent coming up with creative ways to keep the business Anna's mother had entrusted to her afloat.

"I appreciate the gesture, girls, but my birthday is this Wednesday. I doubt we'll be able to schedule a canoe trip on such short notice." Anna latched on to the first excuse she could think of. "Summer is Mrs. Mason's busiest season."

"That's true, but birthdays are special occasions." Sunni waved to someone behind Anna.

"Can you come over here a minute? We have a question for you."

Anna twisted around just in time to see Dash freeze midstep in front of one of the carnival booths a few yards away. He pivoted toward them slowly and made his way to Sunni's side.

"Is it possible Anna and her girls can use their gift certificate this Wednesday?"

Dash didn't respond. Anna wasn't sure if it was because he was trying to stay in character or because Sunni had put him on the spot.

"If you can't fit us in, I under—"

The word lodged in Anna's throat when Dash tugged off his headpiece, revealing the man behind the mask.

The man who'd playfully taken her in his arms and waltzed her through the grass.

The man with tousled, ink-black hair and eyes the velvet blue of a summer evening sky.

The only person who'd seen the bully lurking beneath Ross's charismatic smile.

Liam.

For the last six hours, Liam couldn't wait to remove this silly headpiece so he could breathe fresh air again. Now the only thing he wanted to do was put it back on and pretend he was Aiden pretending to be Dash.

Fortunately, his mom didn't pick up on the tension that thickened the air like an early-morning mist over the river.

"I've been so busy getting things ready for the fund-raiser I haven't had a chance to look at the calendar. Do you know if Aiden is free that day?"

Liam tore his gaze from Anna and tried to dredge up an image of their schedule for the up-coming week.

"He blocked off the day for a private lesson, and Brendan will be out of town for a business meeting."

Liam's pint-size dancing partners, who'd pushed Anna into his arms earlier in the day, wilted like daisies in the midday heat, but Anna looked...*relieved*?

What was that about? Why had she bid on that particular item if she hadn't wanted to win?

"The twins wanted to surprise Anna," Sunni murmured, almost as if she'd read Liam's mind.

"So we kind of forged her signature," Cassie added proudly.

"'Cause it's her birthday," her sister, Chloe, chimed in.

Fortunately for Liam, the girls' names were printed in the center of the giant sunflowers silk-screened on the front of their T-shirts or he would have had a difficult time telling them apart.

"Mom says birthdays don't count when you're her age, but I think they always count, don't you?" Cassie directed the question at Liam.

"Always," he agreed.

"She won't have to do any of the work, either—"

Cassie bobbed her head in agreement. "Mom works a lot—"

"And sometimes she falls asleep on the couch at night—"

"Girls." Anna squeezed the word in, her cheeks flooding with color, as her daughters paused to take a breath. "It's all right. I can call Mrs. Mason and schedule another time."

Instead of agreeing with Anna, his mom tipped her head to one side, something Liam had seen her do whenever she was trying to come up with a solution to a problem.

And then she smiled—at *him*—and Liam knew exactly what that solution was.

Don't say it, Mom.

But she did. Out loud.

"What are *you* doing on Wednesday, Liam?"

Liam made the mistake of glancing at the twins, and the hope blazing in their eyes pulled him in and held him captive like a tractor beam.

"It looks—" Liam heard himself say "—like I'll be going on a canoe trip."

"Gourmet meal. Cooked over an open fire." Liam secured the tie-down on Aiden's canoe and gave it a hard yank. "Seriously?"

"Hey! Take it easy on the old guy." Aiden ran

a comforting hand over the scarlet flames that flowed underneath the curve of the gunwale. "I thought it was a nice touch. Lily claims it's all about marketing, and do you *know* how much swanky restaurants charge for freshly caught trout?"

Liam didn't. And Aiden had to be joking.

"Trout?" He stared at his brother. "I'm going to have my hands full with three inexperienced paddlers, and you expect me to pack a fly rod? And what if I don't catch anything?"

"Huh." Aiden looked a little mystified by this line of questioning. "I guess I hadn't really thought about that. I always catch fish."

His younger brother's confidence, which Liam found humorous if not downright entertaining on most occasions, sawed against his nerves today. "What am I supposed to do? Call Chet and ask him to airdrop a gourmet dinner for four on Eagle Rock?"

Nothing against the manager of the grocery store deli, but Chet's idea of fancy was spackling a layer of ketchup over the tops of the homemade meat loaves before they went into the oven.

"Lily happened to like the description I wrote up for the auction, by the way. She said it was very creative."

That was one word for it.

"Calm water? Sunshine?" Liam stuffed a dry

bag into the bed of the pickup. "You know you can't promise those kinds of conditions."

"It's called setting the right mood." Aiden's eyes narrowed. "And since we're on the subject, what's up with yours? It's not like this will be your first trip down the river."

True. But it would be his first trip down the river with *Anna.*

"I've got two canoes to finish by the end of the week," Liam muttered.

Also true—but a deadline wasn't the reason Liam had been plagued by a series of clips straight from the archives of High School Past ever since he'd gotten home from the shelter's fund-raiser earlier that afternoon.

Past, Liam reminded himself, being the key word here.

Even though Anna, who'd been wearing denim shorts and an apple-green T-shirt when he'd danced with her that afternoon, didn't look much older than the girl who'd breezed up to Liam's locker on his first day at Emerson Middle and High School. She'd had a bright smile on her face and a sheaf of colorful flyers advertising the pep rally on Friday night tucked in the crook of her arm.

Liam had been tempted to go, just so he could see her again, but it didn't take a genius to figure out that Anna Foster belonged to an elite inner circle. Or that Mr. Swanson's fifth-hour study hall would be the closest Liam would ever get to her—and that was only because the seats were arranged alphabetically.

He'd been right. Liam had seen Anna at school practically every day, but it was easy to remember the number of times they'd actually spoken. Once. And that conversation had pretty much destroyed any chance of there ever being a second.

Chapter Three

Anna's hands tightened on the steering wheel when she turned the corner and spotted Liam and Aiden standing in the driveway.

Why had she agreed to this?

Over the past few days, she'd tried to come up with a reason to bow out of their upcoming canoe trip gracefully, but the twins had been talking about it nonstop since the fund-raiser on Saturday afternoon. And in those rare moments of silence when they weren't *talking* about the outing, they'd been preparing for it. Studying the map that highlighted their projected route and memorizing the list of safety tips Sunni had emailed to Anna on Monday morning. Filling out the detailed questionnaire used to determine their level of experience.

On the last page of the information packet, Sunni had added a personal note: "Happy Birthday, Anna! Enjoy the peace and tranquility of a day on the river!"

Peace and tranquility?

Not when Anna's stomach tilted sideways at the thought of spending those hours with Liam.

Regret coursed through her, leaving a bitter taste in her mouth. Words Anna had spoken in anger the night of their senior prom had formed a wall between her and Liam that remained intact even after she'd returned to Castle Falls. Strengthened by time and distance and a silence neither one of them had attempted to break.

But Anna could still see the flash of hurt in Liam's eyes, a sign her words had hit their mark.

What makes you think that my relationship with Ross is any of your business? You don't know the first thing about him...or me. And from what I've heard about your family, you don't know anything about love, either.

How ironic, that *she* was the one who'd proved to be blind when it came to that particular emotion.

A mistake she wasn't going to make again...

"Morning, ladies!" Aiden called out cheerfully. He could have passed for a modern-day river pirate in faded jeans and a black T-shirt with the sleeves cut off at the shoulders. A red do-rag matched the flames painted on the side of the canoe jutting from the back of his pickup truck.

Still, the knot in Anna's stomach loosened a little. She wasn't sure if it was because Aiden was the youngest in the family or because a perpetual gleam of mischief danced in his cobalt-blue eyes, but Anna had always found him to be the most approachable of the three brothers.

Cassie and Chloe obviously didn't share her opinion. They bailed out of the backseat and sprinted across the lawn toward Liam, their copper braids streaming behind them like the tails on a pair of kites.

Anna dragged in a breath, afraid the girls were going to bowl the man right over. But at the last possible second, they skidded to a stop directly in front of him, chattering a mile a minute about their upcoming adventure.

As Anna made her way toward them, she managed to catch every third word or so. Photographs. Sunflowers. Pins and journals.

The average person would have been hard-pressed to make sense of the lilting duet, but instead of clapping his hands over his ears or running for cover, Liam bent closer and gave the twins his undivided attention. A swatch of silky dark hair slipped over his eye and for a moment, Anna saw a lanky adolescent boy slumped in his desk in the back of the classroom.

Rumors had started to run rampant even before Liam and his brothers moved in with the

Masons. Some of the kids said they'd been living on the street. Others claimed that Liam's parents had been sent to prison and the boys would have disappeared into the foster-care system if Rich and Sunni hadn't stepped in and offered them a home.

Anna figured the real story lay somewhere in between, but it was difficult to separate fact from fiction when the people in question refused to speak up on their own behalf.

Brendan, who'd been a sophomore when they arrived in Castle Falls, regarded everyone with barely veiled hostility. He'd stalked the narrow hallway between the middle and high schools with a grungy backpack hooked over one shoulder and a pretty good-sized chip on the other.

Aiden, at ten, didn't sport an attitude, but Anna had overheard Mrs. Harris, the fourth-grade Sunday-school teacher, refer to him as "an active body." A tactful way of saying that Aiden was everywhere at once. Anna had witnessed him crawling under tables and climbing over chairs in the church fellowship room like he was competing in an obstacle course.

And always in the center, like a blue-eyed fulcrum meant to balance the chaos, was Liam. Coaxing a smile out of his older brother. Making sure Aiden's energy was channeled in a positive direction so he wouldn't bump, break or burn something down.

It suddenly occurred to Anna that she'd noticed a lot of things about Liam Kane…

Her heart stuttered like the engine in her cantankerous minivan when her gaze unexpectedly locked with the very grown-up version of the boy she'd been remembering.

"You kids have fun now." Aiden's rumble of laughter broke the silence and he thumped Liam on the arm. "And make sure you do everything I taught you, bro."

Liam rolled his eyes and gave his brother an affectionate shove toward the driver's-side door. "Be safe."

"Where's the fun in that?" Aiden winked at Anna before he vaulted into the cab of the pickup.

Cassie and Chloe obviously saw Aiden's departure as the beginning of their own adventure, because they linked hands and began to hop up and down.

"Can we get our stuff out of the car now, Mr. Kane?"

"Sure, that would be—" Liam stopped.

Because the girls were already gone.

"They can teleport," Liam said.

He sounded so amazed that Anna couldn't

help but smile as her daughters began unloading their backpacks from the back of the van.

"Among other things." Life with twins wasn't for the faint of heart. "Are you sure you're ready for this?"

Was he ready for this?

Ha. Not even close. Not when Anna's smile sent his pulse skipping like a rock over the surface of the water.

Liam reminded himself it had been meant for her daughters, not for him, as he forced himself to meet her gaze.

"Did you have any questions about our itinerary for the day?"

"No." The smile faded. "I think the information Sunni emailed on Monday covered everything."

"Good." So far, so good. "I'll be right back. There's a waiver you'll need to sign—"

"It's in the kitchen." His mom jogged up to them, her pink hiking boots leaving heart-shaped stencils in grass still misted with morning dew. Lily and Brendan's overweight basset hound, Missy, chugged along at her heels. "Right next to the fresh pot of coffee I put on for you and Anna."

Liam reached down to pat the dog, pretending

not to see the questioning frown Sunni tossed in his direction.

Given the fact that Brendan ran Castle Falls Outfitters from an office in their mom's house, it wasn't unusual to do business at the kitchen table, but Liam was anxious to start the four-hour countdown.

He wasn't worried that lingering over a cup of java with Anna in the tiny kitchen would feel awkward. Just the opposite.

He was worried it would feel too *good*.

One more reason to keep his distance.

"Happy birthday, Anna!" Sunni reeled Anna in for a quick hug. "Are you looking forward to spending the day on the river?"

Since Liam already knew what the answer to that question would be, there was no point in hanging around.

"If you have Anna sign the liability waiver, Mom, I'll make sure everything else is ready." He pivoted toward the riverbank, familiar territory where everything made sense.

Where he could breathe air that wasn't laced with the scent of Anna's perfume, a delicate but tantalizing fragrance that reminded Liam of the wild roses that bloomed outside the window of his workshop every summer.

He rounded the corner of the garage, where

he and Aiden shared an upstairs apartment, and almost collided with his older brother and Lily.

"Whoa!" Brendan reared back and pretended to scan the yard. "Where's the fire?"

"I'm on the clock this morning, remember?" Liam reminded him.

Three hours, fifty-two minutes and counting.

"Oh. Right." Brendan linked his arm through Lily's. "Anna Leighton's birthday present. How did you end up playing guide today instead of Aiden? I thought he was the one who came up with the package for the silent auction."

"Aiden had already booked a private lesson."

It was a testimony to Lily's influence that Brendan didn't know the details. BL—before Lily—his brother had micromanaged every aspect of Castle Falls Outfitters, including the things he'd asked Aiden and Liam to oversee. But over the past year, Brendan had loosened his grip and started to focus his attention on marketing and sales, the area of the business he truly enjoyed. Liam was still getting used to this new-and-improved version of his big brother.

"I'm sure Anna will have a wonderful time." Lily smiled.

"She gets to soak up the sunshine and eat food she doesn't have to prepare. What more could a girl want?"

Liam could think of a lot of things.

In high school, it was no secret that Anna couldn't wait to leave Castle Falls. Everyone had expected great things from Emerson's beautiful valedictorian and Ross, the team's talented quarterback. Ross's football scholarship would take the couple through college and then on to places a girl from a small town in the UP could only dream about.

College hadn't been in Liam's future, not when all hands were needed on deck to keep Castle Falls Outfitters out of the red when Rich Mason passed away six months after he and Sunni had opened their home to Liam and his brothers.

As always, memories of his foster dad stirred up a blend of grief and gratitude. Liam still didn't know why God had called Rich home so soon, but the impact he'd had on Liam in those few short months had changed his life.

Where you look is where you go.

One of Rich's favorite sayings chased through Liam's mind. At the time, he'd assumed his foster dad had been talking about paddling a canoe. Any guide worth his salt knew you'd run aground if you kept looking back, but now Liam understood Rich's words of wisdom could apply to a lot of situations.

Like this one.

Which was why he would treat Anna the way he would treat anyone who'd booked a canoe trip with Castle Falls Outfitters. He would be polite. Professional.

Because the here and now was a much safer place to be than camping on the ledge of the past. Or, even worse, allowing himself to dream about the future.

Chapter Four

"Come on, Mom!"

Anna had barely finished signing the waiver on Sunni's kitchen table when the girls burst through the door.

Sunni chuckled at their enthusiasm. "Have a wonderful time. And don't worry about a thing, Anna. You're in good hands."

Liam's hands.

Anna didn't have time to dwell on that. She was taken captive by two impatient little girls who still believed a birthday was a cause for celebration. Not a day to look back on your life and wonder why it hadn't turned out the way you'd expected it would.

The day promised to be exactly the way Aiden had described it on the bid sheet. A whisper of a breeze stirred the tops of the trees, and the sun beamed down at them from a cloudless sapphire sky, turning the surface of the river to glass.

Cassie and Chloe towed her toward the riverbank. Two canoes, fashioned from intricate strips of polished natural wood instead of fiberglass, looked as though they'd come straight from an era when fur traders and lumberjacks roamed the forest.

Anna knew nothing about canoes other than the fact they were supposed to float, of course, but even she could see the craftsmanship that elevated the ones Liam made from the cookie-cutter styles sold in most sporting-goods stores.

Cassie and Chloe could barely contain their excitement while Liam went through the safety procures and demonstrated basic paddling techniques.

"If you don't have any questions," he said after helping the twins put their life jackets on, "I think we're good to go."

"Which canoe is mine?" Cassie wanted to know.

"You and I will share that one." Liam nodded at the canoe on the left.

"It doesn't have flames." Cassie couldn't quite hide her disappointment.

"You saw Aiden's canoe." A hint of a smile came out to play. "A long time ago, my brother found out his name means "fiery," so he painted flames on the sides."

Before the girls could suggest they find a can of paint and decorate *their* canoes, Anna helped Chloe get settled and took her place at the stern.

Liam took the lead and the girls fell silent, their frowns of concentration gradually giving way to awestruck wonder.

The river flowed behind Riverside Avenue, Castle Falls's main street, just steps from the back door of The Happy Cow, but Anna stayed so busy during the day she barely had time to give the picturesque scene more than a passing glance.

Here it cut a sparkling corridor through a hedge of towering white pine, birch and fragrant cedar. The leaves of the hardwoods had slowly unfurled over the past few weeks, opening to a soothing, soul-feeding shade of green. Anna breathed in the scent of sunshine and water and felt something unfurl inside her, too.

The two canoes ended up side by side as they rounded a natural bend in the river.

"Look! Someone is building a playhouse!" Chloe pointed at the skeletal frame of a cabin tucked in a stand of birch trees. Simple lines and the river-rock fireplace rising through the center of the gabled roof gave the structure a rustic charm.

"It's a *house*." Liam chuckled. "I'm hoping to move in by the end of the summer. I work on it in my spare time and Aiden chips in to help whenever he can. He has a vested interest in this place because it means he'll have the garage apartment all to himself."

Cassie's brow furrowed as they drew even with Liam's cabin.

"It's kind of little."

"Cassie!" Anna had taught her daughters to always tell the truth, but while they seemed to understand the importance of honesty, they didn't always grasp the meaning of the word *tact*.

"Well, it is." Cassie stuck to her opinion. "Don't you think it's little, Chloe?"

Ordinarily Anna found it humorous when Cassie attempted to draft her twin sister as an ally, but this time she was too embarrassed by her daughter's candor. Anna discovered it was difficult for a mother to make eye contact and telegraph a silent message while drifting down the river in a canoe.

"It's a *little* little," Chloe agreed.

Liam didn't appear offended or uncomfortable by Anna's daughters' innocent observations. "Just right for one person."

"But aren't you going to get married someday?" Cassie asked, not bothering to hide her shock.

Eight-year-olds—Anna knew this from past experience—didn't hide *anything*.

"And have kids?" Chloe looked shocked, too.

Okay. Family meeting. Tonight. Topic: Personal Questions.

"Girls," Anna finally managed to choke out. "I'm sure Liam knows how big his house should be."

Not according to Sunni.

Liam's mom had questioned the size of the cabin the first time he'd shown her the blueprint, too.

But really, how much space did a guy need anyway? A kitchen. A bedroom. A living room where he could kick back and put up his feet after work.

At least a dozen times a day, Liam pictured how the cabin would look when it was finished. But, suddenly, Anna was there. And not as a visitor. Liam saw her reading in the oversize chair next to the fireplace, her chestnut hair falling loose around her shoulders. Laughing with Cassie and Chloe in the kitchen. Snuggled up with him on the couch while snow swirled outside the window…

Maybe he *should* have asked Aiden to switch places with him today.

Because there was no way Liam would let himself go there.

He thanked God on a daily basis for the blessing of a close family, but that didn't mean he planned to have one of his own.

Maybe if Rich had lived longer, Liam would have had a chance to figure out how to do it right.

He'd heard the rumors about him and his brothers when they'd moved to Castle Falls. Even one of Sunni's closest friends had expressed concern about her ability to handle the household alone after Rich passed away.

Those boys aren't just from a broken home, they're probably broken on the inside, too, Sunni. And you aren't going to be able to fix them with a hug and a smile. Who knows what kind of problems are going to crop up as they get older? They could turn out just like their father.

Darren Kane—a man whose temper had erupted without warning or provocation and inflicted lasting damage on their family—was the last person Liam wanted to be like.

Still, he might have dismissed the comment if he hadn't seen the same concern reflected in other people's eyes.

It made Liam wonder if there wasn't a *fault line*, embedded deep inside of him, a crack formed by the constant upheaval he had experienced as a child. All it would take was a shift of some kind, some unexpected, external pressure, and he'd turn into his dad.

Liam had decided a long time ago it wasn't worth the risk.

For the next half hour, he took a page from Aiden's playbook and pointed out things he hoped Anna's daughters would find interesting. Liam figured he made a poor substitute for his brother, but he kept the twins entertained.

And it kept his eyes focused on his surroundings instead of the beautiful woman sitting in the canoe next to his.

"There's something in the water!" Cassie almost dropped her paddle as she pointed to a sleek brown head moving parallel with the shoreline.

Liam smiled. He no longer needed T-shirts to tell Anna's twins apart. If not for a slight variation in the spray of freckles across their noses, the difference in their personalities gave it away.

Both girls were curious and talkative, but Cassie practically vibrated with restless energy. It was a good thing Liam didn't get motion sickness, because their canoe didn't simply glide down the river—it practically created its own white-water rapids.

"That's Ben." Liam had been hoping the otters would make a guest appearance this morning. He scanned the shoreline. "Keep an eye out for Jerry. They're usually together."

"Ben and Jerry?" It was the first time Anna had spoken directly to him since the start of their journey.

"Aiden named them." Liam smiled. "You of all people know about my brother's addiction to ice cream." Every Tuesday afternoon in the summer, Aiden dragged Liam into The Happy Cow to feed his habit. A triple scoop of Rocky Road.

And every Tuesday, he and Anna pretended there wasn't a barrier ten times higher than the counter between them.

"I see Jerry, too!" Chloe shouted.

"Let's see if we can get them to put on a little show for us." Liam whistled a trio of notes, trying to mimic the greeting Aiden had started using to get the otters' attention when they were newborn pups.

On cue, Ben began to perform barrel rolls in the shallow water, but Jerry, the more courageous of the two, dived underwater and then popped up right between the two canoes, sunlight sparkling on the droplets of water clinging to his whiskers.

The girls squealed in delight as the otter rolled over and exposed his snow-white belly to the sun like a tourist working on his tan.

"Can we take some pictures of Ben and Jerry for my journal, Mom?" Cassie begged. "We'll earn our Celebrate Creation pins, for sure. Josie

Wyman got a picture of a hummingbird, and this would be even better!"

"Celebrate Creation pins?" Liam automatically looked to Anna for a translation.

When the girls had first arrived, they'd said something about Sunflowers and pins and journals, but Liam had had a hard time converting eight-year-old-girl into a language a twenty-eight-year-old guy could understand.

"For the Sunflowers kids' club at church," Anna explained. "The girls earn pins when they memorize Bible verses or complete a special assignment this summer. Except—" She paused to give Cassie a meaningful look. A look Liam recognized because he'd seen the same one on Sunni's face over the years when she was taking advantage of a "teachable" moment. "Except that Ms. Shapiro didn't intend for it to become a competition with Josie Wyman, did she?"

"Nope." Cassie swung her head from side to side, the very picture of innocence. "But I still think it would be sweet to get a picture of the otters for my journal...*and* a pin."

"Mom made them," Chloe added proudly. "She stays up and makes jewelry after we go to bed at night."

Anna's cheeks flushed a deeper shade of pink, but all Liam felt was a stab of guilt. The previous autumn, Lily had rallied the family and a group of volunteers to renovate the second floor of Anna's building into a combination studio and jewelry store. Liam was the only one who hadn't helped with the project.

Given their history, Liam had told himself he was saving Anna from a potentially awkward situation. Now he wondered if keeping his distance had had more to do with *self*-preservation.

Because every time Liam looked at Anna, he remembered the line he'd crossed on prom night. He should have backed off when Anna had gotten defensive, but all he could see was his dad using his fists to get his way.

You need to break up with Ross, Anna. He's dangerous.

Dangerous.

Said the guy everyone assumed had had multiple run-ins with the police before he'd moved to Castle Falls.

You don't know anything, Anna had retorted.

The implication behind the words had struck deep.

Liam didn't know anything because he was an outsider. In Anna's mind, he would always be an outsider. And the knowledge that Liam could have ruined her future happiness if she'd taken his advice was always there, simmering in the air between them.

Which was why it would be better if his relationship with Anna—or lack thereof—stayed the same.

Polite and professional, Liam reminded himself.

"The camera is packed away, sweetheart," Anna said. "I'm not sure we should take the time."

Right. Based on Anna's comment, the four-hour countdown was obviously still on her mind. Proof that she wanted to spend as little time in his company as possible.

Cassie spun toward him, their official river guide and therefore the only person who outranked her mother when it came to making decisions. "Do we have time, Mr. Kane?"

"It's Liam…and you make time for what's important," he told her.

Chloe and Cassie exchanged a disappointed look, so Liam decided he'd better clarify the statement.

"Which means an otter photo shoot just became one of the stops."

Chapter Five

"Yay!"

Chloe and Cassie leaned toward each other and slapped their hands together in a high five that set both canoes rocking.

Before Anna could warn them to sit back down, Liam beat her to it. And he didn't respond with a scold or a scowl, either.

"Rule four," was all he said.

For a bachelor who'd grown up with brothers, the man's patience and easygoing humor with two little girls who chattered more than they paddled was something Anna hadn't expected.

But then again, *Liam* wasn't quite what she'd expected.

Even apart from all the rumors swirling around the three brothers, Anna had always found Liam a little unsettling. There'd been times, during study hall or in the school cafeteria, she'd caught

Liam looking at her. No, not just *at* her. *Through* her. Like he knew what she thinking. Or feeling.

That's what had unsettled her.

But he'd never gone out of his way to talk to her—until the senior prom.

Memories came rushing back. Anna's astonishment when Liam had led her into the center of the gymnasium and then guided her out to the courtyard. Her defensive reaction when Anna discovered the real reason he'd asked her to dance.

I saw what Ross did in the parking lot, Anna. My dad...he wasn't a very nice guy. He would bully my mom like that, too.

Ross wasn't bullying me.

He grabbed your arm.

Anna had denied it even though her arm had still burned where Ross's fingers had bitten through the lacy sleeve of her dress.

Look...just be careful, okay? Liam had persisted. *You don't have to let him treat you like that.*

She'd made excuses for Ross. Told Liam in no uncertain terms to mind his own business.

But she hadn't believed him.

Anna rubbed her arm. The bruises had faded years ago but the wound Ross had inflicted on her heart still hurt.

The theme, A Night to Remember, had fit

as perfectly as the tiara placed on Anna's head when she was crowned queen. But, like so many other moments in her past, that night had become one more thing she wanted to forget.

At least in high school, her wishes and dreams had centered around the plans she and Ross had made for Friday night or on the dress she'd picked out for an upcoming dance. Anna had poured out her heart in a journal similar to the ones Rene Shapiro had handed out to the Sunflowers. Protected her secrets with the turn of a key that fit into a tiny gold lock.

She wasn't willing to take the chance that Liam—or anyone else for that matter—would see the one she kept locked inside her heart.

"Oh, look at that bird over there! Isn't it cute?"

The bottom of Anna's canoe scraped against a rock, warning her that the canoe had drifted into the shallow water. Fortunately, no one seemed to notice she'd broken rule number six—Pay Attention to Your Surroundings—because their attention was focused on the shoreline.

"It's a kingfisher," Liam said. "You can tell by the crested head and the color of his feathers."

"He's making a funny noise." Cassie stopped paddling and Anna could read her mind.

Time for another photo session.

"He's talking to his friends farther down the river." Liam was already reaching for the camera.

"What's he saying?"

"He's saying…" Liam tipped his head to one side and pretended to listen. "Look at those people over there! Aren't they cute?"

Cassie and Chloe giggled, but it was the grin on Liam's face that sent Anna's heart rocking back and forth like a raft caught in a swell.

"It just went under the water!" Chloe exclaimed.

"He's looking for his lunch," Liam said as the bird disappeared underneath the water.

"Lunch." Cassie sounded a little envious.

Her comment reminded Anna they'd been on the river for well over an hour and her daughters hadn't complained a bit about boredom, achy muscles or empty stomachs.

Liam must have realized it had been a while since breakfast, too.

"Is anyone getting hungry?"

"I am!"

"Me, too!"

Liam looked at Anna, and whatever he saw in her eyes seemed to cast the deciding vote.

"Okay, then." He dipped his paddle in the water. "Next stop—Eagle Rock."

Anna had noticed the spot marked on Sunni's map, but until they paddled around a small, tree-lined peninsula jutting out from the shoreline, she hadn't realized Eagle Rock was a…rock.

More like a small cliff, from what Anna could see. It jutted over the river, shading a wide stretch of beach like a sandstone canopy.

As they neared the shoreline, Anna spotted a ring of stones and the blackened remains of a campfire, evidence that Eagle Rock was a frequent stop for paddlers.

Liam, a few lengths ahead of her and Chloe, reached the shoreline first. He hopped out of the canoe, reached for Cassie and deposited her on dry land.

"Are we going to have a campfire on the beach?" Cassie asked hopefully.

"We could…" A smile kindled in Liam's eyes. "But the view is better at the top of the rock."

He didn't mean…

Anna squinted up at Eagle Rock. She couldn't even see a way to *get* to the top.

Before she could suggest they stay on the beach, Cassie and Chloe bumped their fists together and broke into an exuberant little dance right there on the sand.

"Can you take our picture, Mom? When Ms. Shapiro sees how high we climbed, maybe we'll get our Be Strong and Courageous pin, too!" Cassie said.

"We don't know that verse yet," Chloe reminded her sister.

"I do! It's in Joshua. 'Have I not commanded

you? Be strong and courageous. Do not be…'"
Cassie paused, her brow furrowing as she searched
her memory for the rest of the words.

"'Do not be afraid,'" Liam quoted softly. "'Do
not be discouraged. For the Lord your God will
be with you wherever you go.'"

"*You* have to memorize verses, too?"

Cassie's open astonishment brought a smile to
Liam's face again.

"I don't *have* to," he said. "But if you know
what the Bible says, the verses are… They're
kind of like the signposts on the map we gave
you. They keep you going in the right direction.
And if you do get lost…well, they can help you
find your way back, too."

Now it was Anna's turn to stare.

Because she hadn't really expected Liam to
know the verse? Or because the undercurrent
of quiet confidence flowing through the words
told Anna they were stored in his head *and* his
heart?

"I'd be scared if I got lost," Chloe confessed
in a whisper. "'Cause the *bears* might find me."

"I'm not a fan of bears, either." Liam shot
Anna a sideways glance. "Unlike your mom,
who chased one off the high school football field
once."

"A *real* bear?" Chloe clutched Cassie's arm
for support.

Anna had forgotten all about that. And she wasn't sure how she felt about Liam bringing it up now.

"It was a very *small* one," she muttered. "Not much bigger than a cub."

"But still...you chased it." Cassie looked impressed.

"Chased it *away*." Anna shot a look at Liam. "When I screamed."

"She shook her pom-poms at it, too." Liam obviously remembered more about the event than she did. "The other cheerleaders ran inside the school, but your mom stood her ground. Pretty 'strong and courageous,' if you ask me."

Strong? Courageous?

For a moment, Anna wanted to cling to the words even though the girl Liam had just described was long gone.

And the admiration Anna was startled to see in Liam's eyes would be gone, too, if he knew the truth.

When it really mattered, she hadn't been either one of those things.

"Mom was a *cheerleader*?"

The twins appeared more shocked by that information than they were about the bear.

"Your mom made captain our freshman year." Liam couldn't believe Anna had never mentioned it to her daughters. "Her squad won an award for their halftime performance. It was pretty impressive."

"How would you know that?" Anna's eyes narrowed. "You never went to any of the football games."

Liam realized he should have quit while he was behind.

"I…" How to admit this without sounding like a total stalker? "I saw you practice once in a while."

Once in a while meaning every Tuesday and Thursday afternoon, when Liam took a shortcut underneath the bleachers on his way home.

For weeks after he and his brothers moved to Castle Falls, Liam had lived in constant fear that Sunni and Rich would realize they'd made a huge mistake and ship all three of the Kane brothers back to Detroit. Liam would be separated from Brendan and Aiden forever and become a file in some social worker's drawer.

Watching Anna preside over cheerleading practice had been the one bright spot in a day clouded with uncertainty. Outgoing and confident, Anna had had an unquenchable spark of *life* in her eyes and a smile bright enough to light up an entire room. The kind that declared *I'm ready* for whatever was to come.

Only she wasn't smiling now.

When he'd told the humorous story about Anna's encounter with the bear cub, Liam hadn't considered it might resurrect painful memories, as well. The cheerleading award Liam had referred to was displayed in the trophy case, right beside the one Ross received when he'd taken the football team to the state championship.

Way to go, Liam.

Just when he had started to feel like the wall between them was beginning to break down, Liam had reminded Anna what had caused it in the first place.

He pushed out a smile and looked at the twins. "Ready to climb Eagle Rock?"

A loud whoop answered the question.

Liam led the small procession up the winding, overgrown footpath. He couldn't remember the last time he'd climbed Eagle Rock...which told him it had been too long.

It would have been a lot easier to use the fire pit on the beach, but if Rene Shapiro wanted the Sunflowers to celebrate God's creation, Liam couldn't think of a better place than at the top of Eagle Rock.

"How is everyone doing?" He glanced over his shoulder.

Chloe and Cassie gave him the thumbs-up sign, but Anna didn't respond to the question at all. Liam couldn't decide if the climb itself was the problem or if Anna was upset that he'd added at least another hour to the four she had signed up for.

Rocks skittered over Liam's feet as he reached the top of the platform overlooking the river.

His breath caught in his throat, the past momentarily forgotten.

Eagle Rock was more enchanting than he remembered, like an illustration straight from the pages of a fairy tale. A thick carpet of emerald moss covered the ground, and wild grapevine draped the birch trees that circled the sun-drenched clearing.

Cassie scrambled up beside him. And for the first time since they'd launched the canoes, the little girl seemed to be at a loss for words.

It was Chloe who came up with one—a soft, breathless "Wow."

Liam laughed as he set the cooler on the ground. "My brother Aiden discovered this place when we were kids. He stuck a canoe paddle in the ground and made us write our names on it with a rock."

And then they'd rowed back home, minus one paddle, terrified Sunni would ground them—or worse—for leaving the other one behind. She had insisted on accompanying them on the return trip the next day. But, instead of retrieving the paddle, Sunni had picked up the rock and scratched her name next to theirs.

Things had been difficult for all of them after Rich died, but it wasn't until that moment Liam finally began to accept he wasn't alone.

When they got back, Liam had unlocked Rich's workshop and spent the next few weeks paging through his foster dad's notes, studying his designs and slowly figuring out what to do with the strange tools scattered around the room.

Liam had never felt like an outsider in the workshop. For the first time in his life, he'd felt like he was exactly where he belonged.

"Can we write our names on the paddle, too?" Cassie asked.

"I'm not sure I could find it anymore." Liam scanned the thick hedge of trees. "Everything changes from year to year."

Anna, who'd been a few seconds behind them, appeared at the top of the path. And, once again, she carefully avoided his eyes.

Okay.

Maybe not everything.

Chapter Six

"Isn't it beautiful here, Mom?" Chloe threw her arms around Anna's trim waist. "It looks like one of the pictures in the book you're reading to us."

"It is beautiful." Anna's smile didn't quite reach her eyes as she looked at Liam. "How long do you think it will take to get the fire ready?"

"I'm not sure." But not nearly as long as it would take Liam to catch the trout he planned to cook on that fire. "Half an hour or so."

"Oh…" Anna's teeth sank into the plump curve of her lower lip. "I accidentally left my phone in the van. If something happens at work, the afternoon crew won't be able to get in touch with me."

"I have mine. If there's a true emergency, your employees know where you are. They'll call Sunni, and she'll let us know."

"I suppose." Anna didn't look reassured by

Liam's logic. "It's just…I'm sure you didn't plan to spend the whole day with us."

No. He hadn't. But that didn't mean Liam wasn't enjoying himself. Cassie and Chloe were more entertaining than the river otters, and their bright-eyed curiosity reminded Liam of Aiden at that age. And it was nice to see the change in Anna the farther they drifted from civilization. Her slender shoulders had softened into the relaxed pose of someone who'd started to work with the current instead of against it.

She needs a friend.

The thought was too radical to have sprung from Liam's own mind. He'd been a believer long enough to recognize a divine nudge but still… a friend?

Anna had lived in Castle Falls all her life. She was a respected business owner who served on multiple committees at church and in the community.

Not to mention Liam had tried to be her friend once, and it hadn't gone so well.

Mom makes jewelry after we go to bed at night.

Chloe's voice infiltrated Liam's thoughts.

What was that old saying? Out of the mouths of babes?

He studied Anna's face and that's when he

saw it. The faint brushstroke of lavender shadows underneath her eyes.

After Rich died, Liam and his brothers had pitched in to help Sunni. They'd taken care of each other.

But who took care of Anna?

Anna's mother, Nancy, spent the majority of the year in Florida with Anna's grandmother. And for as long as Liam had lived in Castle Falls, Anna's father hadn't been in the picture. For a town with an efficient grapevine, Liam couldn't even remember anyone mentioning him.

Anna worked long hours, and the muffler of her rust-pocked minivan had a plaintive, rasping cough you could hear a block away.

Another nudge.

This one Liam couldn't ignore.

All this time he'd assumed Anna didn't want to spend one minute longer than necessary in his company. But what if she was worried about how much those extra minutes were going to cost? And if she would be the one responsible for paying for them?

"It's my fault we're a little off schedule." Liam strove to keep his tone casual. "If we go over the four hours, consider it a birthday gift from Castle Falls Outfitters."

The flash of relief in Anna's eyes told Liam

he'd hit the proverbial nail on the head even as she started to protest.

"I can't let you—"

"Guide," Liam interrupted, tapping his chest. "Which means you're stuck here until *I* decide it's time to go back."

The girls, who'd been blatantly eavesdropping on their conversation, exchanged a wide-eyed look.

Liam winked at them. "There's another fire pit up here, but we're going to need kindling to get a campfire going. That's where you two come in."

"Okay!"

Cassie and Chloe looked so excited Liam had a hunch they would find some way to connect another Sunflower pin to the mission.

"What would you like me to do?" Anna asked.

"Do you see that rock over there?" Liam pointed to a gigantic piece of sun-warmed sandstone embedded in the carpet of moss. "The one that looks like a recliner?"

A smile tugged at the corners of Anna's lips. "Only Fred Flintstone would look at that and see a recliner."

"That might be true," he allowed. "But I want you to go over there, spread out one of those beach towels you brought along and sit down."

Anna's russet brows dove together. "Sit down?"

"And relax while the girls and I get a fire going."

"Relax?"

Liam tamped down a smile. "I'm paraphrasing a little here, but basically the word means 'take it easy and let someone else do the work for a change.'"

"But—"

"Guide, remember?"

Liam bent closer, so close his breath feathered against Anna's ear and sent a shiver rocketing up her spine.

"I've got this, Anna."

"Here, Mom!" Chloe bounded over with Anna's beach towel, proving her girls didn't miss a thing. "You can use mine."

"Thank you, sweetheart."

Feeling all kinds of self-conscious, Anna trudged over to the rock Liam had pointed out. Slightly bowl shaped with a high back and two slabs the perfect height to rest her arms, it *did* look a little like a recliner.

It took a minute to spread out the towel and another five to get comfortable. A task made more difficult because she was forced to remain idle while her daughters headed into the grove of trees to search for kindling.

"Cassie, Chloe…don't go too far," Anna called out. "Stay where I can see you!"

A shadow suddenly fell across the rock and

momentarily blotted out the sun. Liam stood in front of her, holding what had to be the ugliest hat ever to grace the shelf of CJ's Variety store. It was stained, misshapen and smelled a little like—Anna's nose twitched—*fish*.

"It's pretty bright up here. I thought you might want to cover your eyes." Without waiting for a response, Liam plunked the hat on her head.

"I can't see anything." Anna peered at him through the cloud of mosquito netting that drifted over her face like a pea-green wedding veil.

"It won't matter because your eyes will be closed."

Liam sauntered away to start the fire, and Anna stifled a yawn. Fresh air and sunshine were a dangerous combination for a woman who logged only five or six hours of sleep a night.

She wadded up the towel underneath her head like a pillow and rolled over onto her side so she could keep an eye on the girls.

"I'm going back down and see if I can catch something to eat," Liam announced a few minutes later. "Who wants to come with me?"

Cassie and Chloe squealed and dumped the kindling on the ground beside the fire pit, and were at his side in an instant, not the least bit afraid to take on the wall of rock they'd climbed up a few minutes ago.

Cassie and Chloe loved to play outdoors, but

Anna's childhood home, located on a quiet side street in town, boasted a yard the size of a postage stamp. Anna wasn't ready to let the girls walk to the park alone, so most of their free time was spent in the play area Anna had fixed up in the back room of The Happy Cow or in her studio.

The twins rarely complained, but that didn't stop the guilt from pressing hard against the scar tissue on Anna's heart.

She'd taught the girls how to cook but never over an open flame. They visited the library on the weekends and were halfway through a book about a snowy owl named Winter, while two real-life furry acrobats named Ben and Jerry performed a few miles down the river.

Anna scooted closer to the ledge overlooking the river and stretched out on the grass so she could watch. She'd gone fishing once or twice with the church youth group as a teenager, but the boys had been more interested in catching the girls' attention than catching trout.

The canvas vest studded with colorful lures that Liam shrugged on over his shirt told Anna he took the sport a little more seriously. He retrieved his fly rod from the canoe and walked to the edge of the water. The girls followed, squealing when the ice-cold water lapped against their bare toes.

Anna was used to their exuberant displays of enthusiasm, but Liam was probably wishing he'd taken advantage of the time alone.

Can't you keep them quiet, Anna? How am I supposed to concentrate when they're screeching like that?

Memories from the four years she'd been married to Ross continued to pop up like weeds, crowding Anna's thoughts when she least expected it.

Ross had complained about the level of noise in the apartment, but every sound the twins made had been music to Anna's ears. She'd been terrified Cassie and Chloe would suffer lasting effects from being born a month premature. The girls had been tiny in size and weight, but as the months went by they hit every milestone on the development chart and in some areas, even surpassed other infants their age.

Ross hadn't cared about any of that. He'd been too focused on his personal stats, which had fallen far short of his college coach's expectations for Castle Falls's star quarterback.

Somehow that had been Anna's fault, too.

Ross had been charming and attentive while they'd dated, buying her flowers and candy and saying all the things a girl wanted to hear. And then everything had changed after they'd eloped, making Anna wonder if she'd really known him at all.

She had been too ashamed to tell anyone that her marriage had been far from perfect…and too ashamed to tell Liam he'd been right.

For the twins' sake, she had to protect Ross's memory. And the only way to do that was to keep her secrets.

Liam seemed like the kind of man a woman could trust, but Anna didn't trust her judgment anymore.

She closed her eyes and felt the breeze filter through the lacy holes of the netting as the sound of Liam's husky laughter rolled over her.

The next thing she knew, the girls were screaming.

Chapter Seven

Anna jackknifed into a sitting position, but her view of the shoreline was obscured by a tangle of pea-green netting. She yanked off the hat and clutched it against her chest, but it didn't quite muffle the rapid thump of her heart.

Had she actually dozed off for a few minutes?

Fortunately, no one on the sandy beach below seemed to have noticed. The speckled trout thrashing on the end of Liam's line had captured their attention.

"Liam got another one!" Cassie and Chloe clasped hands and danced around the fishing creel as Liam removed the hook from the fish's mouth. "Now there's one for each of us!"

Anna pushed to her feet and waved the hat to acknowledge Cassie's gleeful shout.

Four trout?

Either Liam was an expert fly fisherman, or she'd been asleep longer than a few minutes.

By the time the three fishermen had retraced their steps up the path and scrambled over the ledge with their catch, Anna had added a few more sticks of kindling to the fire.

"Liam has a secret fishing spot, Mom," Chloe told her. "The trout like to hide there during the day."

"But we can't tell anyone where it is." Cassie drew the tip of her finger across her lips, sealing them shut. For the moment.

"Technically, it's Aiden's secret spot." Liam unleashed a slow smile that rivaled the sun for warmth and sent Anna's heart scrambling for purchase. "But we'll make sure he knows how many we caught."

"Trout fishing is fun, Mom," Chloe said. "You're going to have to try next time."

Next time.

For a split second, Anna let herself imagine another day like this one. Another day with... Liam.

The thought tugged at her heart like the current, but Anna resisted its gentle pull, afraid it would take her to places she wasn't ready to go.

Places she might *never* be ready to go.

She swallowed hard and looked up at Liam.

"Is there anything the girls and I can do while you cook the fish?"

"You can unpack the cooler. Mom said she'd packed a few snacks for us, but when I was lugging this thing up the hill, it felt like she'd packed it with iron ore." Liam flipped open the lid. "And now I know why."

The girls crowded in next to him. "Why?"

"See for yourself." Liam shook his head. "I'm just not sure whether I should be relieved or flattered."

"What do you mean?" Anna's curiosity got the better of her, too, and she moved in for a closer look.

"Mom knows my fishing skills are a little rusty, and she was probably afraid I'd serve you peanut butter and crackers."

Anna's lips parted as she scanned the contents of the cooler. Sunni had taken the description on the silent auction sheet very seriously.

Small glass storage containers were arranged inside the cooler like puzzle pieces, each one containing an entrée of the gourmet meal Anna had been promised. Pasta salad studded with tomatoes, zucchini and pearls of fresh mozzarella cheese. Crispy sourdough rolls swaddled in an embroidered tea towel and a mason jar filled with lemonade. If that weren't enough of a feast, a small but decadent-looking chocolate cake wrapped in fondant and decorated with plump fresh raspberries peeked through the cellophane window of a white bakery box.

"The fish won't take long to cook, so I think we should start with the first course," Liam said.

No one argued.

The twins each claimed a corner of the tablecloth, and when Liam sat down, Cassie reached for his hand.

"We always hold hands when we pray," she informed him.

"My family does the same thing." Liam bowed his head, but he didn't reach for Anna's hand. His fingers lay open, relaxed, giving her the freedom to choose if their family traditions extended to picnics.

Anna hesitated a fraction of a second before she notched her fingers with his. The warmth of Liam's skin, the soft scrape of calluses against her palm, triggered a shiver that rocketed all the way down to her toes.

She slipped her hand free as the twins sang out a cheerful amen.

The fresh air must have affected Cassie and Chloe's appetite, or maybe it was the physical exercise, but they tucked into the food and didn't utter a peep until they were finished.

"The trout was delicious." Anna set down her fork. "But I don't think I can eat another bite."

"Me, either." Cassie blotted her chin with one of the linen napkins Sunni had packed. "Can we have cake now?"

"You just said you were full!" Anna reminded her.

Cassie looked confused by the statement. "I am."

"I think what Cassie means—" Liam winked at her daughter "—is that there's always room for dessert."

Cassie grinned. "Uh-huh."

"Uh-huh," Chloe echoed.

"It looks like I'm outnumbered." Anna gave in with a sigh even though it would have been next to impossible to turn down a piece of chocolate cake.

Liam reached into the cooler and set the dessert down in the center of the tablecloth. Taped to the top of the bakery box was a slender pink-and-white-striped candle.

"I can't remember the last time I had a birthday cake."

Anna reached for a knife, but the girls let her know she was moving through this part of the celebration too quickly.

"You have to blow out your candle first, Mom!"

Liam lit a match and carefully transferred the flame to the tiny candle.

"Make a wish," he murmured.

Inexplicably, tears burned the backs of Anna's eyes as she struggled to think of something.

I wish...I wish I still believed wishes come true.

"So, how did it go today?"

Liam had hoped he could slip quietly into the bathroom and shower off the sand stuck to his scalp—collateral damage from building a castle with Cassie and Chloe after lunch—and retreat to his workshop. But there were his brothers, sprawled on the sofa in the living room.

"Okay."

"Okay," Aiden repeated. "You spent almost the entire day with the beautiful Anna Foster, and that's all you've got?"

"It's Anna *Leighton*, remember?" A fact Liam needed to remember, too. And she *was* beautiful, but that didn't mean he appreciated his kid brother pointing out something Liam had spent the last six hours trying not to notice. Especially when Aiden had become as skilled at charming women as he was at navigating white-water rapids.

"She's a widow now, Liam." Brendan stretched out his legs and snagged a handful of pretzels from the bowl in the center of the coffee table. "Ross has been gone for what...six years?"

Widow. The word didn't fit Anna. Except maybe it did. Maybe grief had cast the permanent shadows lurking in her eyes. Maybe she'd never get over Ross and fall in love again…

"What's with the frown, man?" One of the pretzels in Aiden's hand sailed over the table and bounced off Liam's chest. "I would have thought a morning on the river would have improved your disposition. Didn't you catch any fish?"

"Four rainbow…bigger than the ones you caught last week." Liam knew how to distract his kid brother.

"I want pictures."

"You'll have to ask Anna's twins. They were the ones with the camera."

"The twins." Understanding dawned in Brendan's eyes. "That explains why you're out of sorts. What happened? Did they capsize the canoe? Sing annoying songs all the way to Eagle Rock?"

"No. They didn't. And I'm not out of sorts—" Liam's back teeth snapped together. "The twins are great, okay? Anna's a phenomenal mom, even though it must be hard to do everything on her own."

Where had that come from? And why had he said it out loud?

"Can we talk about something else? Like why aren't you with your wife this afternoon?"

"She and Mom drove over to the animal shelter," Brendan said. "A county deputy called a little while ago and asked if they had room for another boarder."

"Must be a new guy." Aiden grinned. "Otherwise he wouldn't have asked."

His brother was right. It didn't matter if there were no empty kennels available at the shelter. If an animal needed a temporary home, Sunni found one even if she had to coax a friend—or family member—to provide it. The basset hound draped over Brendan's feet, snoring like a rusty chain saw, was proof of their mom's tender heart.

Brendan sighed. "Let's just hope it's something small."

"You think the county deputy found a hamster running loose in the woods? It's probably a litter of Saint Bernard puppies."

"Now I know why Mom's been complaining my cabin is too small," Liam said. "She's already planning on filling up the extra space with stray cats and dogs."

"Right." Brendan drew out the word.

"What is that supposed to mean?"

Aiden grinned. "It means there are other reasons why Mom wants you to add some extra space."

"Dream on. You snore louder than Missy." Liam reached down and scratched one of the basset hound's floppy ears. "You can build your own cabin."

Aiden looked at Brendan. "Is he really that dense or just in deep denial?"

Liam's gaze bounced between his two brothers. "Denial about what?"

"Oh, no." Aiden's hands came up like a shield. "I can't stand to see a grown man cry. You break the news to him, Bren."

"The hard stuff always falls on the oldest." Brendan shook his head. "Aiden means you're next on the list."

"What list?"

"Mom wants all her boys to be happy—"

"Which, in her mind, translates into happily *married*," Aiden interrupted, obviously forgetting his whole I-can't-stand-to-see-a-grown-man-cry statement. "Mission accomplished with son number one—" he aimed the end of his pretzel at Brendan "—so that means Mom has set her sights on number two."

"I'm happy." Liam realized he could have sounded more convincing when Aiden snorted. "Business is going great. I'm going to have my own place. I have creative license in the shop now that my boss isn't being a control freak…"

Brendan ignored that. "That's just it. Mom knows there's more to life than business."

"Said the workaholic."

"*Recovering* workaholic," Brendan corrected him. "Thanks to Lily."

Liam had no idea how a guy could pull off smug and totally smitten at the same time.

"Mom hasn't said anything about my social life." Or lack thereof.

"She didn't say anything to me, either," Brendan pointed out. "And let me just say that Mom isn't above *importing* just the right someone if the situation calls for it."

Which, now that Liam thought about it, was exactly what Sunni had done when she'd hired Lily to give the family home a makeover the previous summer.

Liam had heard their mom claim that she was the reason Lily and Brendan had gotten together, but he'd assumed their mom was teasing.

Now he wasn't so sure. But Brendan had been obsessed with building Castle Falls Outfitters into a successful business.

Sunni had had a right to be concerned. Liam attended a men's Bible study at church. He enjoyed hiking and fly-fishing.

He enjoyed working in the shop, but he knew how to have fun, too.

"I like my life the way it is."

Because it was *his* life.

But who knew what kinds of problems might

crop up as they got older? They could turn out to be just like their father.

The same thought must have gone through Anna's mind.

She hadn't even trusted him with the twins. Liam had seen her perched on the ledge above them, watching when she was supposed to be relaxing.

What did I tell You, Lord? I'm the last person Anna wants—or needs—as a friend.

Liam pivoted toward the door. "I'll be back later."

"Where are you off to again?"

"To spend a few hours on my cabin."

The cabin that was, according to Chloe, "a *little* little."

And perfectly proportioned for a bachelor who intended to stay that way.

Anna crossed the last name off the list and set the church directory back on the coffee table with a sigh.

The two voice-mail messages stored on her cell phone when they'd returned from the canoe trip had welcomed her back to reality with a jolt.

The first one was from Brooke Owens, the teenage girl who watched the girls during the day while Anna was at work. Brooke was on a wait list at a prestigious summer music camp in

Chicago, and a spot had opened up. She had to be there at eight o'clock the next day. Brooke had apologized profusely and left Anna the phone number of a friend she claimed would be happy to fill in until the twins' grandmother returned from Florida at the end of the week.

Except that Nancy Foster, Anna's mom, had decided to extend her stay.

That had been voice mail number two.

Anna's grandmother had tripped on her way to check the mail—no broken bones, her mom had quickly assured her—but Gram had bruised her hip pretty badly and the doctor recommended she stay off her feet for a few days. Anna had returned the call before she'd left Sunni's driveway. Her feisty grandmother had informed Anna the twins needed a babysitter more than she did, but Anna was relieved her mom had decided to make sure Gram was a hundred percent back to normal before she left her on her own.

"I feel terrible!" Nancy said in a low voice when Gram turned the phone over to her again. "I was going to call and wish you a happy birthday and I end up giving you bad news instead."

"You just take care of Gram," Anna had said firmly. "I'm going to make a quick phone call and everything will be fine."

But one phone call had turned into four—and Anna *still* hadn't found a sitter. Brooke's friend

Whitney had accepted a job as a camp counselor and would be leaving the next morning. As Anna had worked her way through the church directory, she'd discovered most of the teenagers had already found summer jobs.

Time to move to plan B.

The stairs creaked underneath Anna's feet as she walked up the stairs, notes to a familiar tune she'd learned as a child.

Every time Anna walked into her old room it felt as if she were taking a step through a time portal. The walls sported a different color, an eye-popping aqua blue instead of the cheerful yellow Anna had chosen when she was the twins' age, but other than that, the room hadn't undergone any major changes over the years.

She pushed open the door, expecting to see the girls sprawled on the braided rug between the beds, playing a board game or building pens for the herd of colorful ponies they'd collected over the years. To her astonishment, they were already in bed. Although, unlike Anna, neither one of them had appeared the least bit tired from having been outside in the fresh air all day.

Chloe was writing in her journal, and Cassie was studying the girls' pink devotional Bible propped on her knees.

At the Sunflowers' first meeting, Rene had given each of the girls a Bible, a colorful bouquet of Sharpie markers and a spiral-bound notebook to record their weekly memory verses. There were also pockets to hold photographs and plenty of blank spaces to capture what Rene called their "doodles and dreams."

"This is a sight a mother doesn't see every day," Anna teased. "Two girls in bed *before* their official bedtime."

"I'm trying to memorize Liam's verse." Cassie's drawn-out sigh had her sinking into the pillow like a bicycle with a punctured tire. "But it's *long.*"

Liam's verse.

Judging from the number of times Anna had heard Liam's name over the past few hours, their guide had made more of an impression than the wildlife they'd spotted along the river.

"We'll work on it together." Anna adjusted the corner of Chloe's bright yellow comforter and sat down on the end of the bed. "You're concentrating pretty hard. Are you working on your memory verse, too?"

"Nope." Chloe didn't look up. "Drawing. So I don't forget."

"What is it that you don't want to forget?"

"Everything." Chloe turned the journal around, and Anna's smile slipped sideways.

Her daughter had sketched a series of pictures,

a colorful collage of their day. Canoes and otters. The campfire. The picnic.

And Liam was in every one.

There was even a picture of his cabin, only it wasn't simply a shell in Chloe's drawing. Smoke curled from the stone chimney. There were flower boxes on the windows, and a puppy that looked suspiciously like the ones waiting for adoption at the shelter sat on a wide front porch.

Anna's throat tightened. "Lights out, now. We all have to be up bright and early tomorrow morning if you're going to work with me."

On the way home, Anna had told Cassie and Chloe about their great-grandmother's fall.

"Work?" Cassie and Chloe exchanged a look of dismay. "Isn't Whitney coming over to play with us?"

"I spoke to Mrs. Burns a little while ago and Whitney isn't available." Anna didn't add that she had already gone through the list of possible candidates and no one was available. "We'll set up a card table in my office tomorrow and you'll have a lot of time to start your next Sunflower project."

Anna tried to inject the right amount of enthusiasm into her voice, but neither one of the girls looked enthusiastic about spending the day inside. She wasn't surprised, given the adventure they'd had that day.

"Now, let's say our prayers and I'll tuck you in."

"Okay." Cassie and Chloe obediently linked hands with Anna.

A smaller circle than the one they'd formed earlier that day. She firmly pushed thoughts of Liam from her mind as she bowed her head.

Prayer time was part of the bedtime routine, but there was nothing routine about Cassie and Chloe's prayers. Nothing was too small to bring to God's attention. Their prayers bounced back and forth like a tennis match. Anna sometimes teased them about God getting a crick in his neck when the Leighton girls knelt by the side of their bed at night.

"Please fix Great-Gram's foot." Following the usual protocol, Cassie started. "And help Mom find someone to watch us until Grandi comes back. And thank you that Mom had fun on her birthday today…and that we got to see Ben and Jerry."

"And that we didn't see any bears today," Chloe added.

"*Or* fall when we were climbing Eagle Rock."

"Liam wouldn't have let us, Cass," Chloe whispered.

"You're right," Cassie whispered back. "Thank you, God, for Liam. And I pray he isn't mad at us for asking personal questions."

Anna and the twins had had that discussion on the way home, too.

"...even though he'd be a good dad because he doesn't yell," Chloe murmured.

Anna's breath tangled in her lungs, making it difficult to breathe. Somehow she got through the rest of the prayer and pressed a good-night kiss against the girls' foreheads before she slipped into the hallway.

She made it to the stairs before the tears began to fall.

Did Chloe remember...*no.* How could she? The twins had turned two only days before the car accident that had claimed Ross's life.

Anna had done her best to protect the girls from Ross's mood swings, which had only gotten worse after the coach benched him for taking a swing at one of the referees during a game.

She'd tried to protect Ross from himself, too. But in the end, Anna hadn't been able to save her marriage or her husband's life.

God...

Anna closed her eyes, wishing she could pray with the childlike faith of her daughters.

But it was hard asking God for help when she felt she'd disappointed Him, too.

Chapter Eight

Liam brushed another coat of varnish on the side of the canoe. He'd been concerned he wouldn't be able to fill their next purchase order, but, at this rate, he'd have it finished and ready to go by the end of the day.

Funny how much a man could accomplish when he couldn't sleep at night. The owl hooting outside Liam's bedroom window was partially to blame...but the rest he assigned directly to the woman with the amber eyes who'd been invading his thoughts over the past two days.

No matter how hard he tried, Liam still couldn't shake the feeling that he should stop by The Happy Cow and make sure everything was all right with Anna.

Because *that* wouldn't get Sunni's attention.

His mom been so interested in every detail of the canoe trip Liam was starting to wonder if there wasn't just a grain but an entire bushel full of truth in Brendan and Aiden's claim.

The number of questions Sunni had asked about the canoe trip had put Cassie and Chloe's curiosity to shame...

The hair on the back of Liam's neck began to prickle.

Twisting around, he spotted two familiar faces in the window. Two familiar *freckled* faces.

He blinked just to make sure he wasn't imagining things. Nope. Still there.

Cassie and Chloe waved at him through the dusty glass. Liam waved back, not realizing they would take that as an invitation to enter the shop.

The door burst open and Cassie reached him first, her feet barely touching the concrete floor as she bounced over the tools scattered on the floor and landed at his side. "Hi, Liam!"

"Hi, yourself." Liam plucked a rag from his back pocket and wiped the varnish off his hands. "I didn't expect to see you two out here today."

Cassie's grin showcased the gap between her two front teeth. "Did you miss us?"

The question landed with the force of a punch to Liam's midsection.

Because, strange as it seemed, he *had* missed them. The laughter and the constant questions and the...togetherness...had filled a hole Liam hadn't known existed. He'd missed Anna, too.

The tiny frown that settled between her brows when she'd navigated the canoe around the rocks. Her rare smiles, as unexpected and mesmerizing as shooting stars.

A guy could get used to all that. Even a guy who'd discovered the quiet life he'd spent years cultivating had started to feel too quiet over the past few days.

While he was recovering from that unexpected epiphany, Chloe suddenly pressed her hands to her mouth.

"A *cat*." She breathed the word and flopped down onto her knees beside the cardboard box underneath Liam's workbench.

Cassie dropped beside her and stifled a squeal. "And kittens!"

"Yup." Five of them, although from the amount of destruction they'd left in their wake over the past forty-eight hours, sometimes it seemed like there were a lot more of the little fur balls.

Liam tried to keep them corralled while he worked but a two-foot wall of cardboard had proved to be a flimsy barrier against the kittens' endless quest for adventure.

"They're so cute." Chloe propped her chin on her hands, thoroughly enchanted by the long-haired gray-and-white cat nursing her babies in a nest of plaid flannel that had, in a former life, been one of Liam's shirts.

"How old are they?"

"I'm not sure." But old enough to knock Liam's radio off the workbench right in the middle of one of his favorite George Strait tunes, sharpen their tiny claws on a roll of plastic and wage a full-scale attack on the cord of his power sander.

Their mother must have realized her offspring were out of control because, in lieu of rent, she'd deposited a dead mouse on the mat outside the door of Liam's shop that morning.

"Can I hold one?" Cassie peered into the box.

"It's up to Big Kitty." Liam bent down to scratch the mama cat's white chin. "She's the one in charge."

Cassie and Chloe collapsed in a fit of giggles that roused the kittens from their nap and sent them ambling over to greet the new visitors.

"Okay…what did I say that tickled your funny bone?"

Liam's question seemed to have the same effect, but Cassie recovered first. "Her name is Big Kitty?"

"She's the biggest one, right?" Liam figured she would appreciate his logic.

"I think you should call her Feathers," Chloe crooned, reaching out to stroke the mama cat's plume-like tail. "Because she's so soft."

A cat named Feathers.

"You can call her whatever you'd like," Liam said. "She's only here until my mom finds homes for her and the kittens."

He still wasn't quite sure how he'd ended up playing foster dad, but Sunni promised it would be a temporary assignment.

She'd also promised the kittens wouldn't be any trouble.

But after two days trying to keep track of the furry criminals, the litter of Saint Bernard puppies Brendan had joked about Sunni bringing home might have posed less of a challenge.

"You could keep them." The absolute certainty in Chloe's big brown eyes had Liam scrambling to remember all the reasons he *couldn't*.

"No, I… No." He picked up one of the kittens, a tiny replica of its mother, and carefully placed it in Chloe's arms.

"I'm pretty busy and these little guys need—" *round-the-clock surveillance* "—more attention than I can give them."

Cassie sighed. "That's what Mom always says, too."

"We could help you." Chloe buried her nose in the kitten's downy fur. "We're on summer vacation."

Liam knew that, but it still didn't explain why the twins were *here*. Unless Anna had made plans to get together with Lily. They would have seen each other at their weekly book club meeting the night before, though, which meant...

You're way too familiar with Anna's schedule.

"Is that why you stopped over?" Liam teased. "You're going to sign up for another canoe trip and earn those Strong and Courageous pins?"

"Nope!" Cassie shook her head so vigorously that her copper braids locked together. "Grandi had to stay in Florida to help out Great-Gram—"

"'Cause *she* fell down and hurt her hip."

Liam was getting better at following the twins' unique way of finishing each other's sentences. "Grandi is your Grandma Nancy?" he guessed.

"Uh-huh. That's why Mom brought us to work with her today,"

Cassie said. "Brooke is in Chicago and Whitney was supposed to watch us, but she got a job at a summer camp and she's probably having way more fun than us because *she* gets to go swimming and hiking and we'll have to stay inside all day."

"Cass." Chloe gave her twin a disapproving frown.

"Well, she is." Cassie's chin lifted. "And we will."

A niggling suspicion began to form in Liam's mind. "When did all this happen?"

A frown creased Chloe's forehead and he could

see her going backward in time, counting the days. "When we got back from the canoe trip."

That explained Anna's expression when Liam had carried the twins' backpacks to her van. She'd been standing by her van, cell phone in hand, and the worried look on her face had worried *him*.

But when Liam asked if everything was all right, Anna had looked him right in the eye and told him that everything was fine.

It stung a little, knowing she hadn't confided in him. Then again, why would she? She didn't owe him an explanation.

"Girls? Where are you?"

Anna's voice drifted through the screen door and the guilty look that passed between the twins told Liam they didn't have their mother's permission to seek him out.

"They're in here," Liam called back.

A heartbeat of silence passed and the door opened.

Liam still didn't know what had brought Anna back to Castle Falls Outfitters but she must have come straight over from work. A few tendrils of chestnut hair had escaped the confines of her ponytail and she still wore her uniform, a knee-length denim skirt and a white, short-sleeved shirt with an ice-cream cone embroidered on the front pocket.

Liam thought she looked stunning. And a little embarrassed when she spotted Cassie and Chloe sitting on the floor by his workbench.

"Look at the kittens, Mom!" Chloe carefully held up one for Anna's inspection. "Aren't they cute?"

"Yes, they are," Anna agreed. "But didn't I tell you and your sister to wait for me by the van?"

"We did." Cassie's bright smile eclipsed the sunlight streaming through the window. "It's parked right outside."

Anna decided she was going to have to be more specific with her instructions.

The butterflies stirring in her stomach when she'd heard Liam's voice took flight when he ducked his head to cover a smile.

He looked...different...today. And not only because he wore a heather-gray T-shirt and a tool belt that hung low on the hips of his faded jeans. Liam had been at ease paddling a canoe down the river, but, here, surrounded by the tools of his trade, he appeared completely at home.

And in the few short moments Anna had left the twins alone when she went to find Lily, they had certainly made themselves at home, too.

Anna should have known they would seek out Liam. On the drive over to Castle Falls Out-fitters, Cassie and Chloe had chattered nonstop about the canoe trip. Anna had nodded and hummed in agreement at the appropriate times but she didn't have the luxury of dwelling on the past when the future of her high school class reunion was in jeopardy.

Courtney Meade had barged into The Happy Cow five minutes after Anna had unlocked the door that morning. Anna had taken one look at her former classmate's face and known that Courtney hadn't given in to a sudden, overwhelming urge for an ice-cream sundae. She and Courtney had performed in several theatrical productions while they were in high school, and, after serving on the reunion committee with the woman over the past six months, it had become increasingly clear that Courtney hadn't outgrown her love for drama.

Only this time, Courtney had had a valid reason to be upset. While standing in line at the deli counter—and eavesdropping on a conversation between the women in front of her—she'd realized the pavilion Anna had rented for the reunion had been double-booked for the Fourth of July weekend.

Anna had immediately called Marty Jensen, the chamber president, who apologized for the "clerical error" but claimed there was nothing he could do.

Leaving Anna approximately two weeks to

find an alternate venue. And in a town the size of Castle Falls, it wasn't as if there were a whole lot of options. The closest county park was twenty minutes from town and didn't have running water, electricity or a place to take shelter if it rained. Anna had gone so far as to contact Elaine Turner and ask if there was any way they could split the time at the pavilion, but the Turner family picnic was an all-day event.

A sigh slipped out before Anna could stop it.

"The girls told me about your grandmother." Liam's husky voice washed over her. "Is she doing all right?"

Gram. The latest family crisis had been on Anna's mind all day, too. She forced herself to meet Liam's eyes.

But she wasn't prepared for the genuine concern she saw there. For a moment, Anna was tempted to tell Liam how difficult it was to be so far away from her family when something like this happened. Tempted to lean against one of those broad shoulders and absorb some of his strength…

Unnerved by the wayward path that thought could take her down, Anna managed a jerky nod, instead.

"The doctor wants Gram to go in for a follow-up next week and make sure everything is healing the way it should, but she claims she's fine."

"What about you?"

Anna was spared from having to answer the question when the door swung open and Lily breezed in.

"I'm so sorry, Anna! Here I asked you to stop over after work and then I'm not even around when you get here."

"That's all right." Anna tried not to let her confusion show. The cryptic message Lily had left on Anna's phone had sounded urgent, but Lily didn't look distressed. As a matter of fact, her friend looked a little...triumphant. "You said you needed my help with something?"

"Actually...I think I might be able to help *you*." Lily winked at the twins. "I heard a rumor that you're looking for a new place to hold your class reunion."

Anna gaped at her. "You did?"

She'd lived in Castle Falls for the majority of her life, but the speed—and efficiency—of a small-town grapevine never ceased to surprise her.

"I overheard Courtney talking about the mix-up when I stopped by the coffee shop this morning." Lily's eyes twinkled. "And I think I have the perfect place for you to hold your class reunion."

"Really?" Anna latched on to the words like a lifeline. "Where?"

"Right here."

"Here?" Anna echoed.

"Bren and I have been brainstorming ideas to build the business over the past few months," Lily said. "And one of things we'd like to do is partner with the community for special events."

All Anna heard was one word.

Partner.

She glanced at Liam. Was it her imagination or did he look as stunned as she was by Lily's offer?

"We've got plenty of space for whatever you need," her friend continued. "And if you think about it, we can offer a lot more perks than the pavilion!" Lily began ticking off items on her fingers. "You'll have access to our canoes if someone wants to take a jaunt down the river, the use of the horseshoe pits and outdoor kitchen. Whatever you need we'll do our best to provide."

It sounded too good to be true.

It also sounded expensive.

Courtney, whose responsibilities included keeping track of the class checking account, guarded every penny as zealously as Olivia Thorne, the owner of the coffee shop, guarded her recipe for white chocolate raspberry scones.

"The committee has a pretty small budget to work with," Anna murmured. "What would you charge?"

"The same amount you would have paid to

rent the pavilion," Lily said promptly, another clue that she and Brendan had discussed the idea at length before she'd left the voice mail on Anna's phone. "You'd actually be doing us a favor. We weren't going to rent out the grounds for events until next spring, so your reunion will be a testing ground of sorts. A chance for us to work out any kinks in the plan."

The confidence in Lily's voice told Anna she didn't really expect there to be any.

"It's such short notice, though," Anna stammered. "I'm sure you have a full schedule without adding my class reunion to the mix."

"We are pretty busy this time of year," Lily admitted. "But if your committee helps us get things in order, I know it will turn out great."

Everything about Lily's idea sounded great. Except…

Anna was the one in charge of the details. The point woman for getting things in order.

And Liam was included in the "us" Lily had mentioned.

"All you have to agree to right now is a tour," Lily said. "Take a walk around the grounds and see if it will work for you."

Anna swallowed hard. Agreeing to let Castle Falls Outfitters host the reunion did seem like the perfect solution to her problem, but she could think of another one she didn't dare voice out loud.

A ruggedly handsome, blue-eyed problem who was well on his way to winning the hearts of two little girls.

And who made Anna's pulse beat a little faster every time he smiled.

But hadn't she prayed on the way over that God would provide an alternate venue?

"All right."

Chapter Nine

Liam released a breath he hadn't even realized he'd been holding.

His ten-year class reunion. Now the reason Lily had invited Anna over became clear. Anna had been on student council all four years of high school and class president their senior year.

Her name and address were stamped on the RSVP envelope Liam had received along with his invitation several months ago. Both were still pinned to the bulletin board above his desk, right next to a receipt for a new saw and a photograph of Aiden posing with his canoe at Stoney Creek Camp, one of their most loyal customers.

"Sunni and Aiden are on board." Lily turned her attention to him now. "All we need is Liam's vote and it will be unanimous," she added brightly.

One of the kittens pounced on Liam's hiking

boot, and he reached down to untangle its claws from the laces, grateful for a moment's reprieve.

Brendan and Lily had brought up the idea of renting out the grounds for community events, but Liam hadn't realized they'd moved beyond the initial planning stage.

His sister-in-law's influence again. Before Lily's arrival in Castle Falls, his older brother had come up with creative ways to avoid "connecting" with people in the community.

Back in the day, the Masons' property had been the go-to place for church picnics and day-long floats down the river. Rich and Sunni had wanted to share their love of the outdoors with everyone they met, so it wasn't unusual for the couple to focus more of their attention on people than they did on the amount of money the business brought in.

But, after Rich died, Brendan was the one who'd said they could keep the business going if they built canoes instead of renting them out. His brother wouldn't admit it, but Liam suspected there had been another motive, one that had nothing to do with fiscal responsibility, behind the suggestion. Building the canoes and shipping them to buyers had cut down their face-to-face interaction with certain people who lived in Castle Falls, too.

People loved Sunni and it was no secret that

some of her friends had encouraged her to turn Liam and his brothers over to the foster-care system when she became a widow. For Brendan, the knowledge had cut deep, leaving room for bitterness to take root in a heart already damaged by the years they'd lived in Detroit.

Sunni had agreed with Brendan, but, knowing their adoptive mother, she'd been more concerned about giving Brendan time to heal than she was about finding the time to make more canoes.

Lily cleared her throat and Liam realized she was still waiting for him to cast his vote.

"It's pretty short notice." Liam was careful not to make eye contact with Anna. "I'm not sure we're ready for something like that."

Oh, who was he kidding? Liam wasn't sure *he* was ready for it. He'd tried to make peace with the past, but reliving his high school years? Not exactly his idea of a good time.

Lily didn't seem the least bit put off by his honesty. "Well, there's only one way to find out!"

Her optimism was one of the things Liam appreciated the most about his brand-new sister-in-law, but, at the moment, he could think of at least a dozen obstacles standing in the way of their success.

The reunion committee had scheduled the event over the Fourth of July, a decision Liam guessed was meant to accommodate former classmates who'd moved away from Castle Falls but returned to visit family in the area for the holiday. As an added bonus, they could take advantage of the festivities the local chamber of commerce had already planned for the weekend.

Now he flicked a quick look at Anna and saw a reflection of his own doubts in her eyes.

Was she concerned about changing the entire venue on such short notice? Or was she afraid Castle Falls Outfitters wouldn't be able to pull off an event like this at all?

At least Anna couldn't blame Liam if it didn't meet her expectations. Brendan and Lily wouldn't expect him to be involved in planning the details *or* carrying them out.

The door swung open again and Sunni bustled in, her smile as wide as Lily's. "I heard that someone is here for a tour of the property!"

Word traveled fast. Liam expected it would only be a matter of time before Aiden sauntered into the shop to say hello to Anna, too.

"It's really generous of you to let us rent your property on such short notice," Anna said.

"You're going to be thrilled with everything Lily has in mind!" Sunni said. "We've been tossing ideas back and forth all afternoon. You can talk about them while you look the place over."

Liam couldn't help but notice his mom was the one who looked thrilled.

"I'm not sure I have time for a tour today," Anna said slowly. "I still have to put in a few hours at the studio this evening and I'm sure the girls are anxious to get home and stretch their legs for a little while first."

"Well, that's a shame, because I just took a pan of chocolate-chip cookies out of the oven and I could use a test taster." Sunni winked at the twins. "Although two would be even better."

Cookies must have ranked second underneath kittens because the girls' faces lit up and they jumped to their feet.

"We can stretch our legs when we walk back to the house, Mom." Cassie aligned herself with Sunni and the taste testing team.

"Chocolate-chip cookies are best eaten warm," Sunni said.

"And I'm sure Liam wouldn't mind showing you around."

Wait a second.

He wouldn't mind?

Liam stared at his mom in open disbelief. She returned the stare with an innocent smile. She was good. He'd give her that. But Lily—Anna's friend *and* the marketing expert who'd come up with the idea to host community events—would come to his rescue.

"That's a terrific idea! Liam is way more familiar with the grounds than I am." Lily was halfway to the door before Liam could protest. "I want to track Aiden down and ask him when he's going to start on the volleyball court, anyway."

The volleyball court? If Liam hadn't heard about that, chances were he didn't know what other plans his family had concocted while he spent the days holed up in the workshop.

"Thanks, Liam!" Cassie skipped toward the door while Chloe carefully transferred the kitten she'd been cuddling into Liam's arms.

"I'll be back." She planted a kiss on its downy head. "Be good."

Everyone filed out the door—some faster than others, Liam couldn't help but notice—and the door snapped shut.

Sealing him and Anna inside.

Anna wasn't sure how it had happened, but suddenly she and Liam were alone in the workshop. And without the buffer of the twins' constant chatter, silence swelled between them. It was broken by Liam's quiet exhalation, which Anna could only assume expressed his feelings about being forced to act as her guide for the second time in less than a week.

"I'll be right back," Liam said, and Anna found herself holding the kitten as Liam disappeared through a doorway in the back of the room. "I have to…check on something."

That was fine with her. Because she needed a moment to get her emotions in check. Anna's relief over finding an alternate place for the reunion hadn't replaced the new knot forming in her stomach at the thought of spending more time in Liam's company.

She set the kitten on the floor so it could play with its siblings, but the animal seemed to be more intent on exploring its surroundings. It pounced on a sunbeam and batted a scrap of wood across the floor like a tiny hockey puck. When the wood chip vanished underneath a table in the corner of the room, the kitten followed its prey without hesitation.

A split second later, Anna heard a tiny sneeze, followed by a pitiful meow.

"Got yourself into trouble, didn't you?" She knelt down, extracted both kitten and wood chip, and searched for something to wipe off the dust that clung to her hands.

Anna scanned the contents scattered on top of the table and realized it served double duty as Liam's desk. Drawings of canoes covered almost every square inch of the surface, and a heavy ceramic coffee mug weighted down a stack of envelopes. The bulletin board attached to the wall behind it was crowded with family photographs and old newspaper articles.

His invitation to the class reunion.

The deadline to sign up was yesterday, but Anna couldn't remember seeing Liam's RSVP card in the mix. She lifted the corner of the invitation, peeked underneath it and realized why.

He hadn't sent it in.

The card hadn't made its way to the mailbox yet, but it was clear Liam had already made a decision. An X marked the little box beside the words *Not Attending*.

Anna shouldn't have been surprised. Other than worship services on Sunday mornings and the occasional outing with his family, Liam tended to avoid social gatherings. Anna had heard people call him "aloof" and "reserved," but the man who'd taken them out on the river Wednesday had revealed a playful side that seemed at odds with the description. And his patience had extended far beyond the number of questions that two curious girls were able to come up with during a four-hour canoe trip.

But men can be good at pretending, Anna reminded herself.

When Ross had had an audience, he could be funny and charming. He'd been Castle Falls's favorite quarterback, and he'd quickly won over his college teammates, as well. Ross knew how to play to a crowd. It was only behind closed doors that Ross had allowed his temper to show.

After they were married, she'd become his scapegoat. The person Ross blamed whenever something went wrong.

Liam emerged through the doorway with a bowl of fresh water. He set it down in front of the mama cat before turning to Anna.

"So…tell me more about the reunion."

"You're not going." The words tumbled out before Anna could stop them.

Liam glanced at the bulletin board and Anna realized she'd just admitted to snooping. Fortunately, he didn't call her on it.

"I guess I am now, seeing that it's going to be held in my backyard."

"Good." Anna nodded briskly. "I'll add your name to the list then."

"According to Bren and Aiden, it's already there," Liam muttered.

"What?"

"Never mind." Liam's lopsided smile almost made Anna forget why keeping a safe distance between them was the smartest thing to do. "How many people are you expecting will attend?"

"Fifty responded yes, but there are always a few who sign up at the last minute."

"Fifty." Liam looked astonished by the number. "That's almost our entire graduating class."

"It's our first reunion. I'm sure people are anxious to find out what everyone is doing now." Anna hadn't seen many of her classmates since she'd eloped with Ross, but many of them had reached out with cards and phone calls when they'd heard about the car accident that had taken his life.

Ross had been Castle Falls's golden boy, destined to shine, and Anna had stood proudly at his side.

What would her classmates say if they knew Ross had pushed her away in the months before he'd died? That he'd blamed Anna that his football career had ended before it had barely begun...

"Anna?"

With a start, she realized Liam had asked her a question.

And now there were a dozen more rising in his eyes.

What had he seen on her face?

"Sorry," Anna murmured. "What did you say?"

"You're going to need a tent."

"I know." Anna added another item to her to-do list. "I'll call the hardware store and see if they have one available that weekend."

"I can do it."

"But—"

"Consider it part of the package." Liam reached down, picked up one of the kittens and returned it to the box with its mother. "If Mom doesn't find a home for these critters, I'm going to fund the entire addition for the animal shelter myself," he grumbled.

"I thought they belonged to you."

Liam winced. "This is temporary until she finds a good home for them."

"You didn't happen to mention that to the girls, I hope."

"I might have." Liam smiled for the first time. "But I'm sure Mom already has some adoptive parents in mind. She has this uncanny way of knowing who needs a pet. Even if *they* don't know it." He crossed the room to the back door and held it open so Anna could exit first.

She stepped onto the concrete stoop and saw an entire fleet of fiberglass canoes moored together in a sea of freshly mowed grass.

"You made all of these?" Anna had had no idea the business was doing so well.

"Aiden and Bren help out if I need them. These are one of our most popular lines. We ship them to camps all over the Midwest so I make sure there's enough to cover any extra orders that come in."

"What about the canoes we took out on the river? The ones that look like the model in the showroom? Do you make a lot of those?"

It hadn't seemed to bother Liam when Anna mentioned the invitation for the class reunion, but now his brows hitched together over the bridge of his nose.

"I get a few orders from people who appreciate the vintage design, but it's hard to justify spending hours on one canoe when every sale counts," he said after a moment. "All that the majority of our customers require is that their canoes float and come with a reasonable price tag."

"I know what you mean. Except for the floating part," Anna added. "Customers who complain they can buy less expensive jewelry never quibble about the price of an ice-cream cone. It makes me wonder if I'm focusing on the wrong business."

Why had she told him that?

It was one of the doubts that continued to plague Anna since she'd taken the leap and opened her studio almost a year ago. Even her mom, whose opinion she respected, had expressed some misgivings about Anna's decision to turn her weekend hobby into a business.

"Maybe you are."

The words cut deeper than they should have. Anna turned away, wishing she'd never brought it up, but Liam stepped in front of her, blocking her escape.

Liam's gut clenched when Anna flinched.
Whoa.
He stepped back, opening up a wider space between them.

"I was talking about The Happy Cow," he clarified. "Why don't you lease out the lower part of the building and focus your time and energy on what you love?"

"It's not that simple." Anna's gaze slid away from him. "The Happy Cow has been a family-owned business for years. My mom...and Gram...they're counting on me to keep it going. What if you told Sunni and your brothers that you didn't want to build canoes anymore?"

Liam didn't even have to think about it. "They would understand."

"But...wouldn't they be disappointed in you?"

"*In* me?" Liam tipped his head, not sure what Anna meant. "I think they'd only be disappointed if I felt God was leading me down another path and I didn't follow. Have you talked—"

"There's no point." Anna reached into her purse and pulled out a notebook and pen, all business again. "I can do both."

Liam was going to ask if she'd talked to *God* about it, but he took the hint and let it drop. It was clear Anna didn't want to talk about it anymore. At least not with him.

They walked in silence to a spacious clearing near the river. Late-afternoon sunlight filtered through the leaves of the trees, creating stencils on the grass. Four orange stakes that hadn't been there a few hours ago marked the spot where the future volleyball court would go.

"What's the time frame we're looking at?" Liam had skimmed through the invitation the day it arrived. He remembered the reunion was on Saturday afternoon, but he hadn't really paid attention to the details. They hadn't mattered because he hadn't planned on attending.

"We're going to meet at two o'clock—that will give people an opportunity to watch the parade—and then we'll have a few hours before dinner to catch up." Anna bent her head to jot something down in her notebook, and a tendril of chestnut hair escaped from her ponytail. "Lily mentioned volleyball and horseshoes, and Courtney has some special activities planned. We might want to have a bonfire before the community fireworks start."

"The bonfire is doable. Aiden put in a fire pit a few years ago and you can see the flames from Canada."

"I'm sorry to put you to so much trouble." Anna frowned, and Liam stuffed his hands in the front pockets of his jeans on the off chance he did something stupid. Like reach out and smooth away the lines that had settled on her brow. "Holding the reunion at the pavilion would have been a lot easier."

It would have been easier on him, too.

"I suppose that's it for now." She slipped the notebook back into her purse. "It was sweet of Sunni to give the girls a snack, but I don't want to take up any more of her time."

His mom was sweet, but Liam's brothers had him doubting it was Sunni's only motivation for the offer.

The smell of warm chocolate greeted Liam as they followed the sound of laughter to the kitchen. The twins sat at the table with Lily and Brendan's basset hound camped on the floor between them, ready to catch any crumbs that fell. Sunni was flitting around the room, and Liam guessed it was the presence of the children and not sugar that had increased the spring in her step.

"So...what's the verdict, Anna?" Lily topped off Chloe's glass with a splash of milk.

"I think it will work."

"Great!" Lily held out a plate piled high with chocolate-hip cookies. "We'll make the change a smooth transition for you, Anna. I promise. You have enough on your mind so I don't want you to worry about the reunion, too."

"Cassie and Chloe told me about your grandmother, Anna," Sunni said. "I'll be praying for a speedy recovery."

"Thank you," Anna murmured. "Mom is worried Gram won't follow the doctor's orders and rest, so she wants to stay a little longer."

"I miss Grandi." Chloe dunked a piece of cookie into her glass of milk. "She takes us to the park and does fun stuff with us."

Cassie released a gusty sigh. "And she promised to help us earn our Sunflower pins."

"Did you find someone for park-and-pin duty until she gets back?" Lily, who'd been loading cookies into a plastic container, paused to glance at Anna.

"There seems to be a babysitter shortage at the moment." This time, Anna's smile didn't reach her eyes. "The girls will have to come to work with me. I have a play area set up in my office for emergencies like this. We'll be fine."

Cassie and Chloe didn't contradict their mother, but the dejected slump of their shoulders spoke volumes. Liam imagined that trying to keep Anna's adventurous twins occupied in her tiny office would be as challenging as keeping five kittens happy while confined to a cardboard box.

Lily must have thought so, too, because she frowned. "Since we'll have to meet a few times to discuss the reunion, why don't you leave the girls here with me during the day until your mom gets back?"

"What?"

Liam realized he and Anna had spoken at the same time.

"I couldn't—"

"I think it's a wonderful idea," Sunni interrupted. "I could use some dog walkers at the shelter, too, and I heard the Sunflowers are pretty good helpers."

Cassie and Chloe popped up in their chairs like bobbers. "We are!"

"It's all settled then." Lily handed Anna the container of cookies. "I'll swing by the ice-cream shop tomorrow morning and bring them back here until you get done with work."

"But tomorrow is Saturday," Anna protested, her gaze bouncing from Lily to Sunni and back again. "I'm sure you already have plans for the weekend."

"Not a thing!" Lily said. "But I'm sure Cassie and Chloe will help us come up with something. Won't you, girls?"

"Uh-huh." Cassie and Chloe grinned.

At Liam.

He knew Anna didn't stand a chance against

two cheerful steamrollers like his mom and sister-in-law, but Liam had a sneaking suspicion that *he* was the one in trouble.

Because when the twins nudged each other, Liam had a sneaking suspicion that Cassie and Chloe—by accident or by design—were the newest recruits on Sunni's matchmaking team.

Chapter Ten

Anna had flipped the Closed sign propped against the window of The Happy Cow so it faced the street and glanced at the clock.

She'd planned to run home and freshen up before she drove out to Sunni's house to pick up the girls, but a trio of women dressed in clothing more suited to walking down a New York fashion runway than the network of hiking trails near Castle Falls had swept into The Happy Cow before she'd had a chance to lock the door.

Given the time of day, Anna had assumed the women were searching for something a little more substantial than ice cream to eat. The Happy Cow did have a few tables for customers to relax with their ice cream but it lacked the kitchen space for a grill, and sit-down restaurants were few and far between in the area, but the number of disappointed looks Anna received from tourists when they discovered The Happy Cow didn't have a full menu had prompted a conversation with Olivia next door. The local coffeeshop owner—an artist in her own right when it came to creating masterpieces out of humble ingredients like eggs, butter and flour—personally delivered a batch of enormous, salt-encrusted pretzels fresh from the oven over to The Happy Cow on her lunch break. It was first come, first serve, of course, and because the locals knew exactly when Olivia took said lunch break, the pretzels were usually gone by midafternoon.

Anna had worked up a smile and inwardly braced herself to share the bad news about the lack of restaurants, but the oldest of the three women hadn't so much as spared a glance at the chalkboard on the wall behind the counter that listed the flavors of ice cream. She'd announced they were looking for Anna's Inspiration and the GPS on her cell had brought them—she'd held up the device as proof—*here*.

Anna had experienced a moment of sheer panic when she realized the women's jewelry matched, in both quality and price, the tiny gold labels attached to the designer bags looped over their shoulders.

But she'd inhaled a deep breath, exhaled a silent prayer and ushered them upstairs to the second floor.

The absolute silence that followed had distilled Anna's insecurities into a full-fledged case of outright panic…and sent visions of one-star reviews dancing in her head.

The oldest of the three women had smiled and glided into the room, but her friends hadn't exerted the same control. They'd worked their way from display to display, enthusiastically oohing and aahing over the bracelets and lingering over the necklaces as if they were choosing penny candy from the variety store on the corner. They'd also helped themselves to Anna's newly minted business cards, each one finding a home in the sleek inner pocket of a trendy leather bag.

The women had finally drifted out the front door, leaving Anna with a seven-minute window to drive over to Sunni's house and pick up the twins.

Cassie and Chloe had been awake and dressed before the alarm clock went off that morning, excited about spending the day in what Cassie announced was "our new favorite spot."

It hadn't crossed Anna's mind until she'd returned to The Happy Cow what her daughter might have meant by the statement. She could only hope it was the river and not Liam's workshop.

One more reason to hurry…

The door rattled and Anna contemplated ducking behind the counter to avoid another last-minute customer.

"Anna?"

A muffled voice—a *familiar* voice—froze her in place.

Anna slowly turned toward the door. She wasn't imagining things.

Douglas and Barbara Leighton—her former in-laws—were standing on the sidewalk.

Had she missed something? A card? An email? Because her former in-laws hadn't warned—*told*—Anna they were coming for a visit.

Another rattle. "Aren't you going to let us in?"

Anna realized that if she could see Ross's parents, they could see her, too. She rushed over to open the door.

"Surprise!" Barbara kissed the air near Anna's cheek. "You weren't at home, so Douglas and I took a chance you might still be here."

Ross's father wasn't a touchy-feely person, so Anna gave him a smile instead of a hug. "How was the drive up?"

"Long." Douglas's gaze swept over the interior of the dining room. "Did you finally decide to take my advice and extend your summer hours?"

If Anna extended her hours, the girls would be eating supper while they got ready for bed.

"No, I still close at six, but some customers

snuck in and asked if they could see the studio before they checked into the bed-and-breakfast."

"Studio?" Barbara looked confused.

"Anna's Inspiration. My jewelry business?" The one Anna had mentioned in her emails. "I've had quite a few orders since my website went up."

"You actually went through with that?" Ross's father, who'd been Castle Falls's only attorney before accepting a partnership in a prestigious law firm located in Grand Rapids, had a way of staring a person down as if they were on the witness stand. "Wouldn't it have been a bit more prudent to find out if there's a demand first?"

"My friend Lily helped me. She worked at a marketing firm, and she's the one who helped me create a business plan."

Douglas let the topic drop, but Anna had a feeling the conversation wasn't over. Her father-in-law had earned a reputation for biding his time and waiting for the right moment to strike.

"Where are my granddaughters?" Barbara's smile faded as she looked around. "I thought they'd be here with you."

"My grandmother slipped and fell a few days ago, so Mom decided to stay in Florida until Gram can get around a little better on her own," Anna explained. "Cassie and Chloe are over at Sunni's house today."

"Sonia Mason?" Douglas's brows slid together over the bridge of his nose, and Anna wished she hadn't mentioned that last part. She had never understood her father-in-law's animosity toward a woman the rest of the community loved, but whenever someone mentioned Sunni's name, the man's expression turned chokecherry sour. "Is the canoe business doing so poorly she had to take in extra work?"

"My friend Lily is the one who offered to keep an eye on them for me. She and Brendan were married a few weeks ago."

Douglas's scowl only deepened, and Anna turned to Barbara before he could voice his opinion of Sunni's adopted sons.

"How long will you be staying in Castle Falls?"

"I'm not sure." Barbara stooped down and picked up a tiny piece of napkin Anna had missed when she'd swept the floor.

"We'll be driving to Escanaba for a few days to visit some friends but plan to be back on the weekend. It always takes a few days to freshen things up and make the cabin livable again."

The Leightons' "cabin" was a year-round, four-bedroom split-log home with a hundred feet of frontage on a private lake. They hired a caretaker to keep up with the yard work and stock the refrigerator before they visited in the summer.

Anna, who'd grown up in a modest two-story

home, had been in awe the first time Ross had invited her over to watch a movie after a football game. The Leightons had spared no expense when it came to their only child. They'd even converted an outbuilding into a gym so Ross could stay in shape for football during the long winter months.

The best brings out the best, Anna had heard Douglas boast to his friends in the bleachers.

Anna sometimes wondered if that was one of the reasons Ross's father had been so angry when he'd found out she and Ross had eloped. Douglas hadn't wanted anything—or anyone—to distract Ross from his goal of making the pros after college. When Anna had moved from being Ross's high school sweetheart to his wife, Douglas's attitude toward her had changed.

"Cassie and Chloe will be sorry they missed you," Anna said. "Maybe we can get together after church tomorrow?"

Irritation flashed in Douglas's eyes. "Barbara and I planned on taking you and the girls out for dinner tonight."

What about *her* plans?

As soon as the thought formed in her mind, Anna felt a pinch of guilt. She'd called the other members of the reunion committee over the weekend to give them a brief update and they'd had some questions they wanted Lily to address when they met that afternoon. But the Leightons only returned to Castle Falls a few times a year and even though they didn't have a close relationship with Anna, she knew they missed their grandchildren.

"I'm sure Cassie and Chloe would love that," she said. "They've been begging me to take them out for pizza since school let out."

"We already made reservations at Twin Pines," Douglas said.

"It's the only restaurant in the county that can make a decent steak."

Twin Pines was also a half-hour drive from Castle Falls. By the time they drove home, it would be too late for Anna to return phone calls for the reunion committee. Or work on the necklace an online customer had commissioned as an anniversary gift for his wife.

"Should we pick up Cassie and Chloe while you go home and change clothes?" Barbara's gaze lit on a smear of hot-fudge sauce decorating the pocket of Anna's apron.

"No." Had she said that too quickly? Given Douglas's reaction to Anna's choice of a babysitter, she didn't want to take the chance he would say something to Sunni that might offend her. "If the girls have been playing outside all day, they'll have to change their clothes, too."

"All right." Douglas consulted his Rolex. "We'll pick you up at the house in twenty minutes."

"I can't wait to hear about the birthday present the girls got you," Barbara called over her shoulder as Douglas ushered her toward the door. "They were very secretive about it. The only thing I could get them to tell me was that it was something you needed."

The door closed behind them and Anna sagged against the counter.

Something she needed.

A day on the river wasn't a gift Anna had been able to hold in her hands or place on a shelf in the house, but every moment had lodged in her heart and taken up residence there.

Sunlight sparkling on the water. The girls' laughter as Liam caught a trout. The warmth of the campfire.

And a verse that continued to play in the background of Anna's mind over the last few days, reminding her that God was always with her. Truth that had somehow gotten buried under the weight of Ross's anger and accusations.

And Liam…

She had to stop thinking about Liam before he worked his way into her heart, too.

There was no room for him. Not with all the secrets Anna carried there.

* * *

Liam heard the low, unhappy growl of a muffler seconds before Anna's minivan turned down the driveway.

Cassie heard it, too. "Mom's here!"

"Shh." Chloe sat cross-legged on the floor, surrounded by sleeping kittens. Ten minutes ago they'd been performing the feline version of Cirque du Soleil in his work space.

Liam caught a glimpse of Anna through the window as she walked toward the house. Because she assumed the twins would be with Lily. The woman who'd offered to keep an eye on them. But Lily had ended up taking a phone call that had somehow consumed the entire afternoon, and Sunni had had an emergency at the animal shelter, which left only one person in the family who was available to step in.

Him.

Liam jogged to the door and poked his head out before she reached the front steps.

"Anna?"

She froze. Slowly turned to face him. "I'm late picking up the girls."

"They're with me."

Anna retraced her steps down the flagstone walkway. "Where is Lily?"

Matchmaking from afar, Liam was tempted to say. But he couldn't make an accusation like that without solid proof. "On the phone with a customer, but I'm expecting her back any minute. And a water pipe broke at the shelter, so Mom had to drive over there and wait for a plumber," he added, anticipating Anna's next question.

"I hope the girls didn't stop you from getting something accomplished."

"Nope." Liam had actually gotten a lot accomplished.

Anna slipped past him into the workshop, and he heard her suck in a breath.

Oh, yeah. He probably should explain the reason her daughters' clothing was splattered with paint, too.

"Hi, Mom!" Cassie flew to Anna's side. "We had so much fun today. Liam—"

"Is going to call Lily and find out what's taking so long." Liam reached for the cell phone in his back pocket. "A few questions came up when we were talking about the reunion last night, and she wanted to discuss them with you."

Anna was already shaking her head. "I won't have time tonight. We have plans for dinner."

"Pizza!" Cassie broke into a little jig.

"Not this time, sweetheart. We're going to Twin Pines."

Cassie's nose wrinkled. "But that's a *quiet* place."

"Your grandparents are here for a visit and it's the place they chose."

Douglas and Barbara Leighton. Liam struggled to keep his expression neutral. When Les Atkins accused Brendan of stealing his watch shortly after they'd moved to Castle Falls, it was Douglas Leighton who'd counseled Les's father to press charges. Even though he was innocent, Brendan ended up being suspended from school for a week.

But that wasn't enough for Atkins. Les and his friends had continued to make life miserable for Brendan until they'd graduated. The day Rich had suffered a heart attack, Les claimed Brendan had spray-painted profanity on the wall of the gymnasium. Brendan had been taken into police custody and charged with vandalism. Fortunately the truth had come out, and eventually Brendan's name had been cleared.

Not that it had swayed public opinion. Brendan had been labeled a troublemaker, and since the same blood flowed through Liam and Aiden's veins, they'd been judged guilty, as well.

It had taken years to earn the respect of the community, but Liam knew there were some people who would always view them as outsiders. Douglas Leighton was one of them.

"Do we have to go right now?" Chloe couldn't quite conceal her disappointment as she rose to her feet, careful not to wake the kittens sprawled on the floor.

"Yes, we do." Anna eyed the flecks of blue paint

interspersed among Chloe's freckles. "Grandpa and Grandma will be picking us up at the house, and you'll have to get cleaned up before we leave."

That was his bad.

Liam raked his hand through his hair. "I'm sorry, Anna. I had no idea that paint *did* this. Let me just state for the record that mine stayed on the brush."

The corner of Anna's lips trembled, and Liam would have jumped headfirst into a vat of paint if it had coaxed that tiny smile into full bloom.

"What were you painting?"

"We'll show you, Mom!" Chloe grabbed Anna's hand before she could protest and dragged her over to the lopsided Dr. Seuss-like structure behind Liam's workbench.

They'd devoted the better part of the afternoon to the project. Liam had created two towers from wood and pieces of bright yellow carpeting, and linked them together with a tunnel made out of plastic ice-cream buckets. He and the twins had discovered some cans of leftover paint from Lily's home makeover the summer before, but the girls couldn't decide what color to paint the boards. So they'd used all of them.

"It's a…" Anna paused and studied the curtain of feathers dangling from strips of leather over the entrance of the tunnel.

"A—"

"Playground." Chloe came to her rescue. "Liam said the kittens needed something to keep them busy while he was working on his boat."

"The kittens?" Anna stared at Liam over her daughter's head.

Liam stared right back. "That's right."

"And now we'll get our Caring for God's Creatures pin because the kittens have a place to play." Cassie slipped her arm through her mother's. "Did you make that one yet?"

"I did." Anna smoothed Cassie's hair away from her forehead and uncovered a splotch of yellow paint. "Okay. Grab your backpacks, and let's get going."

"But we have one more thing to show you!"

"How long *was* Lily's phone call?" Anna said under her breath.

Three...four hours. But, because it sounded like a rhetorical question, Liam didn't say so out loud.

The twins towed Anna into a room adjacent to Liam's shop, a holding cell for an eclectic collection of odds and ends no one quite knew what to do with.

"Sorry about the mess." He pushed a box aside with his foot. "Now that we're expanding into day trips again, Brendan and Lily have big plans for this space. Once I get the shelves up, we're going to stock them with camping equipment and snacks and use it as a check-in point."

"They're going to call it The Trading Post." Cassie pointed to a brand-new paddle hanging from brackets on the wall. "All the people who rent canoes get to sign their names, and Liam let us be the first ones!"

"'Cause they're starting a new tradition and we were the first explorers of the season," Chloe chimed in.

"That was very nice of you," Anna murmured.

So why wouldn't she look at him?

"Lily would call it good marketing." Liam tried to ease the sudden tension by cracking a joke. It only worked for Aiden, apparently, because Anna's gaze dropped to the floor.

Had he done something wrong? Other than give two eight-year-olds free access to the paint cabinet, of course.

I don't know what to do, Lord. I want to be Anna's friend, but this "one step forward, two steps back" thing is hard.

"You can sign your name, too, Mom," Chloe said.

"Another time." Anna tapped her daughter's button nose. "If we don't scrub this paint off, you're going to have to wear it to the restaurant, and your grandparents will think you and Cassie joined the circus."

"Your mom is right." Liam might fail at DIY projects with third-grade girls, but he remembered the Leightons well enough to know that—for them—image was everything.

"Bye, Liam." Cassie locked her arms around Liam's waist and hugged him. "Don't forget to take pictures of the kittens."

Chloe was next. "Bye, Liam! I'll see you Monday."

Now Anna did look at him. And she appeared as shocked as Liam by the twins' unexpected display of affection.

As he watched Anna shepherd the girls out the door, Liam had the sinking feeling they'd taken another gigantic step backward.

But that didn't stop his thoughts from taking a dangerous little side trip as Liam imagined what it would be like to hold Anna in his arms.

Chapter Eleven

Anna left the van running as she hopped out of the driver's seat on Monday afternoon.

She was running late. Again.

Over the past twenty-four hours, it seemed there'd been one crisis after another. Anna had taken a shift in the church nursery during the worship service the day before and then driven the girls to the park for a picnic lunch afterward. In between loads of laundry and responding to an avalanche of emails from Courtney regarding the reunion, she'd discovered one of the freezers at the ice-cream shop had died. Anna had called the electrician's emergency number only to discover he didn't *handle* emergencies on a Sunday evening.

He'd promised he would be there "as soon as he could" on Monday, which ended up being half an hour before The Happy Cow closed for the day.

On her way to pick up the twins, Anna could feel fatigue spreading through her bones.

Once the reunion was over, things would get better. Her mom would be back in Castle Falls. The teenagers Anna had hired for the summer would be trained and ready to take control of a shift, freeing up some of her time.

Life would settle back into its normal routine.

Anna, who'd never thought of herself as a person who thrived on routine, could definitely see its benefits. It was predictable. *Safe.*

It didn't include a quiet, blue-eyed man who had somehow managed to earn her daughters' affection—and trust.

Even Chloe, the more cautious of the twins, had hugged him goodbye on Saturday.

In spite of what he'd claimed, Anna knew that Liam hadn't put aside his work to help the girls with a project because he'd needed something to keep a litter of stray kittens occupied. And letting Cassie and Chloe sign the canoe paddle wasn't merely good marketing, either. Both were the actions of a man who paid attention to the needs of others.

Cassie and Chloe were sweet natured and friendly, but Anna had never seen them take to someone the way they'd taken to Liam. They barely knew him and yet they'd hugged him as if he were a lifelong family friend.

Or part of their family.

That's what scared Anna the most.

Cassie and Chloe were getting way too attached to Liam, and she didn't want them to be heartbroken if he suddenly decided his life would be easier without two little girls underfoot.

Anna had been tempted to call Lily that morning and tell her the girls were spending the day at The Happy Cow, but Cassie and Chloe were buckled in the backseat before Anna had finished putting on her makeup. To sentence them to a day inside would have risked a mutiny. Especially when the girls wouldn't understand why their mother had changed her mind at the last minute.

A burst of laughter snagged Anna's attention before she reached Sunni's front door. She veered down the stone walkway and followed the sound to the back of the house.

At least the twins weren't in Liam's workshop this time.

"We're in here, Anna!" Lily's lilting voice came from the three-seasons room overlooking the river.

Anna opened the screen door and had to sweep aside a curtain of crepe-paper streamers before she entered the room.

"Hi, Mom!" Chloe stood on a wooden chair

in front of a poster taped to the wall, a bouquet of Magic Markers clutched in her hand.

Clusters of balloons decorated each corner of the room, and someone had woven a string of lights around the ancient ceiling fan. A popular, upbeat praise song played in the background, adding to the festive atmosphere.

Cassie and Lily were in the process of hanging more streamers from the doorway that separated the three-seasons room from the rest of the house.

"We're helping Lily decorate." Cassie abandoned her post for a moment and ran over to give Anna a hug.

"I see that." Anna's arms closed around her daughter, and she breathed in the sweet scent of orange-blossom shampoo. "What's the occasion?"

"It's a birthday party…kind of."

Now Anna felt even worse. "I'm sorry I'm late picking up the girls again, Lily. There was an issue with one of the freezers, and I had to wait for an electrician to show up."

An electrician who'd informed Anna the cost of replacing the parts on an appliance that old would be almost as much as buying a new one, but she kept that information to herself.

Lily waved aside her apology. "Don't worry about it. I loved having two extra helpers."

"How is your grandmother doing, Anna?" Sunni swept in, carrying a Crock-Pot that instantly filled the room with a delicious aroma. "The women in my morning Bible study prayed for her today."

Anna wasn't surprised the news of her grandmother's injury had reached so many. Gram had lived in Castle Falls all her life, and even though she'd been in Florida the past few years, she still kept in contact with her friends.

"Thank you." Tears stung the back of Anna's eyes and she blinked them away before anyone could notice. "I called Mom last night, and apparently Gram is still pretty sore. She doesn't seem to be bouncing back quite as fast as the doctor thought she would."

"Bones take time to heal." Sunni set the Crock-Pot on the table.

"She learned that from me." Aiden sauntered through the doorway. "Four trips to the ER."

"Five."

Anna's heart plunged to her toes when Liam entered the room behind his brother. He must have walked over from the shop. Sawdust clung to the front of his T-shirt, and once again a tool belt dipped low on his hips, but the rugged attire—coupled with a two-day growth of stubble shading his jaw—only made him look like he'd stepped off the pages of an outdoor magazine.

"I'm not counting the appendectomy," Aiden informed his brother. "That wasn't my fault."

Liam cocked an eyebrow. "Prove it. It got you out of shoveling snow for a month."

Sunni clucked her tongue. "Shush, you two, and say hello to Anna. She's going to think I never taught you boys any manners."

"Hello to Anna." Aiden reached for the lid of the Crock-Pot and dodged out of Sunni's way when she tried to swat his hand.

He gave her a mischievous wink and Anna couldn't help but smile. "Hi, Aiden."

"Anna." Liam's eyes met hers.

Life, she thought, wasn't fair sometimes. Aiden's roguish smile didn't affect her in the least, but all Liam had to do was say her name and her heart started beating in triple time.

"Hi, Liam."

An awkward silence stretched between them, only this time it was fallout from a situation spanning two days instead of ten years.

"Okay." Sunni clapped her hands and looked around the room in satisfaction. "I think everything is ready to go!"

And so were they.

Anna turned to Lily. "It looks like you've got plans for the rest of the day, so tomorrow we can go through the checklist for the reunion."

"Not so fast!" Lily swiped a folder from a

wicker end table. "I have an email receipt in here for the tent, and the manager of the rental company threw in a few folding tables for free. There's also a portable generator to hook up a sound system if you need one."

Anna flipped through the contents of the folder. "I can't believe you got this much accomplished already." Lily had cut Anna's workload in half. "I guess we can go over the decorations for the theme when I get off work tomorrow."

She took two steps toward the door and realized her troop wasn't falling into line behind her.

"We can't go yet, Mom," Cassie wailed. "Sunni and Lily invited us to stay for supper."

"And we're having strawberry shortcake for dessert." Chloe took up the refrain—different words, same tempo. "With whipped cream."

"You can't say no to whipped cream." Aiden's wide grin put him on the girls' side.

Oh, yes. She could.

"It was very nice of Sunni to invite us, but it wouldn't be polite to intrude on a family birthday celebration." Anna pressed down on the word "polite" to remind the girls they'd covered this topic in the past.

"Technically, it's our adoption-day party," Aiden explained. "Sixteen years ago today, Sunni signed the papers that made us a family."

"God made us a family." Sunni's smile frayed

a little at the corners. "The paperwork made it official. And we would love to have you and the girls celebrate with us, wouldn't we, Liam?"

It hadn't escaped Anna's notice that Liam was the only one in the room who hadn't tried to convince her to stay.

Sunni must have noticed, too.

"Mom's right. You should stay." Liam backed toward the door. "And I'd better start the grill."

"Liam is our resident chef," Sunni said. "He's the only one with the patience for it."

Lily cleared her throat, and Anna realized everyone in the room was looking at her. Looking at her looking at *Liam* as he left the room.

Aiden flashed a grin at Cassie and Chloe. "What do you say we tag along and watch him? My mom always says I need more patience."

"Our mom tells us that, too!" Cassie told him.

Anna suppressed a groan as the girls skipped out the door behind Aiden.

Over the course of the day, she could only imagine what else the girls might have told them.

"You can run, but you can't hide."

Liam sighed and made a mental note to fix the lock on the door of his workshop. "I'm not hiding. I'm looking for...something."

Brendan propped his shoulder against the door frame. "Your courage?"

"Maybe." Liam surprised them both by admitting it.

"I felt the same way when I realized I was falling for Lily."

"I'm not *falling* for Anna." Liam closed the drawer on his toolbox with a little more force than was necessary.

The word conjured up images of sweaty palms and a rapid heartbeat. Being so tongue-tied, it was difficult to speak.

Liam wasn't suffering from any of those things...

Okay, maybe the rapid heartbeat.

But Liam was afraid the *falling* part had happened years ago and his heart had simply been biding its time, patiently waiting for his head to catch up.

"Uh-huh." Brendan didn't look convinced. "I seem to recall saying those exact words a few times, too."

It wasn't the same.

His brother had fought his attraction to Lily in the beginning, but the only obstacle to their happiness had been Brendan's rigid adherence to his calendar. When it came to pursuing a relationship with Anna, *Liam* was the obstacle.

What did he have to offer someone like her? Anna hadn't dated anyone since she'd returned to their hometown.

In high school, he hadn't been able to compete with Ross Leighton on any level. Now that Ross was gone, Liam couldn't compete with his memory, either.

"I also seem to recall drifting off into space and not responding when people were talking to me."

Liam snapped back to reality. "What?"

"You just proved my point."

"Do you need something? Or did you just come here to annoy me?"

"Both." Brendan pushed off the door frame. "The twins were looking for a tree to climb—something about a Strong and Courageous badge—"

"Pin." Liam glanced out the window. Dusk had fallen while they'd demolished an entire batch of Sunni's strawberry shortcake. Frogs trilled in the reeds, and the campfire Aiden had started after dinner cast a rosy glow on the faces of the people standing in the yard.

"Anyway… Mom suggested I ask if you can rummage up a few extra flashlights for firefly tag."

Liam wasn't prepared for the avalanche of memories that came rushing back.

"Firefly tag? We haven't played that since…" *Rich passed away.* "Since we were kids."

"Well, Anna's twins have never played it, so Mom thinks it would be the perfect time to learn."

Liam cocked a brow. "*You're* going to play firefly, too?"

"Lily has never heard of it, either," Brendan grumbled.

"I'm not sure I have a choice."

The first time Rich had suggested they play, fifteen-year-old Brendan hadn't been exactly open to the idea then, either.

"Games are for kids," he'd scoffed.

Another adult might have pointed out the fact they *were* kids. Not Rich Mason.

Liam put aside his momentary irritation with his oldest brother and grinned. "Do you remember what Rich said when you refused to join in? *You have to play. If you don't, your brothers will be short a musketeer.*"

Rich had dubbed them the three musketeers after they'd arrived in Castle Falls because he "respected men who had each other's backs." Liam had warmed to the idea—no one had ever given them a nickname other than "those Kane boys" and the word "respect" hadn't come up in those conversations, either.

Brendan had scoffed at that, too, but Liam had seen a copy of the book sticking out of his backpack a few days later.

Looking back, Liam realized what a gift their

foster dad had given them that night. He and his brothers had learned to survive, but the Kane household, with its lack of light and love, had never been an environment that encouraged things to grow.

Rich, a quiet mountain of a man in plaid flannel and worn denim coveralls, had explained the rules, handed out flashlights and turned his foster sons loose in the woods. And then, because he was a man who led by example, he had joined in the mayhem.

Liam hadn't even cared about winning. He'd flopped down behind a tree, flashlight clutched against his chest, and soaked in a sound he hadn't heard in a long time. His brothers' laughter.

An expression Liam couldn't quite define crossed Brendan's face. "I remember," he said gruffly. "Now quit stalling, or Mom is going to send out a search party for the search party."

Liam snagged a few flashlights from various hidey-holes in his workshop and followed Brendan outside. The sun had already started to set, but he could make out the silhouettes of the people standing in a loose circle, waiting for their return.

Anna sat at the picnic table, content to watch from the sidelines instead of joining in the fun.

What was up with that?

Was he the only one who realized how much

Anna had changed since high school? She'd always been in the thick of things, surrounded by people drawn to her effervescent personality and megawatt smile.

Liam had been one of them. But for a twelve-year-old boy who'd been in a dark place most of his life, staring at Anna was like looking directly at the sun. So he'd kept his distance.

Cassie and Chloe jumped up and down and cheered when they saw him approach. "Liam's going to play firefly tag, too!"

"These two are going to be easy to find," Aiden murmured.

Sunni shushed him as Brendan explained the rules of the game.

"One person is it, and the rest of us are fireflies." His brother flicked his flashlight on and off a few times to demonstrate. "The object is to hide, flash your light three times and then run away before you're caught. If you're caught, you get put in the jar."

"The picnic table," Sunni clarified in a whisper.

"You have to stay there until the game is over—unless another firefly is brave enough to try and rescue you." Brendan emphasized the word *try.* "Any questions?"

"You forgot one of the rules," Liam said.

"I did?" Brendan frowned. "Which one?"

"*Everyone* has to play." Liam didn't look at Anna. His brother was smart, right? Everyone meant everyone.

"I don't re— *Ouch!*" Brendan pressed his hand against his side, kneading the spot where Lily's elbow had sunk in.

"Sorry." Lily flashed a bright smile. "Mosquito."

"Come on, Mom!" Chloe was already tugging a reluctant Anna from her perch on the picnic bench.

Anna shot Liam a look—which he ignored.

"I have a question!" Cassie's hand shot up. "Who's going to be it?"

"I will." Liam volunteered, because Brendan was extremely competitive and Aiden lightning fast. Knowing his brothers, the game would be over before Cassie and Chloe had a chance to hide.

Sunni checked to make sure the flashlights were in working order before she handed them out.

"Ten…" Everyone scattered toward the woods when Liam started the countdown. By the time he opened his eyes, he stood alone in the yard. "It looks like a good night to catch some fireflies," he called out, repeating the line Rich had bellowed the first time they'd played.

A light flickered in the bushes, followed by

a ripple of laughter. Aiden hadn't been off the mark when he'd said the twins would be easy to find. Liam veered in the opposite direction. A stick crunched underneath his foot, and a feminine squeal punctuated the darkness a few feet away.

"Hi, Mom."

"Ack!" Sunni's protest drowned out the chirp of the frogs.

"How did you know it was me?"

"Um…because you always pick the same hiding place?" Liam flipped on her flashlight and used it to guide his mom over to the picnic table.

Chances were if he found Lily, he'd find Brendan, too. The newlyweds would stick together while Aiden worked his way from tree to tree until he reached the shed by the river.

In this game, the darkness worked in everyone's favor, but Liam remembered his family's favorite hiding spots.

A half hour later, Anna was the only one who'd eluded capture.

"Help us, Anna!" Aiden shouted. "You're our only hope!"

Liam rolled his eyes and slapped at another mosquito as he peered into the shadows at the edge of the trees. A light flashed…*there*!

Liam crossed the distance in a heartbeat. It helped that he knew the woods so well he could find his way through them blindfolded. But there was no Anna. Just a flashlight, propped against a mountain of pine needles.

Which meant… Anna had outsmarted him.

But she couldn't outrun him.

Liam retraced his steps and caught a glimpse of Anna running in a course parallel to his as she wove through the trees, her goal the picnic table.

Oh, no, you don't.

Anna didn't see Liam as he closed in on her. And Liam didn't see *her* change directions to avoid a patch of marigolds Sunni had planted to fill a bare spot in the yard until it was too late.

They hit the ground together in a tangle of arms and legs.

Liam felt a tremor roll through Anna's body, and he levered onto one elbow and searched her face.

"I didn't mean to tackle you!" He brushed a strand of hair from Anna's cheek. Her skin felt like satin, just the way he'd imagined it would. "Are you all right?"

Anna nodded mutely, her breath coming out in short, uneven gasps that drew Liam's attention to her lips. Ignoring the internal alarms that began to sound, Liam lowered his head.

Anna's lashes drifted closed…

"Hey! What's going on over there? Did you forget about us?"

Aiden's laughter brought Liam back to his senses. He hadn't only forgotten about them—he'd forgotten everything.

He'd forgotten that he had no business even *thinking* about kissing Anna, let alone acting on the impulse.

But reality came crashing back when she rolled away from him and stumbled to her feet.

Chapter Twelve

Anna pressed a hand against her chest, but the rapid thump of her heart wasn't a side effect from her mad dash across the lawn.

When she and Liam had collided, he'd shifted his weight a split second before they hit the ground and used his body to cushion her fall. Anna could still feel the imprint of Liam's warm hands on her sides. Heard the ragged hitch of his breath in her ear…

Now *she* was the one having trouble breathing.

Had Liam moved closer so he could make sure she wasn't hurt…or had he been about to *kiss* her?

Suddenly aware they had an audience, Anna took a wobbly step toward the picnic table.

And then another.

Liam rose to his feet but kept a careful distance this time. "Anna—"

"Just give me a minute," she wheezed. "I have to…win."

Liam's expression changed from wary to disbelieving as Anna sprinted toward the picnic table. A cheer went up from the captives as she ran a circle around it, slapping each one of the captives' outstretched hands to make it official.

"I can't believe you did that!" Lily sang out from the midst of the captives Anna had set free.

"I'll bet Liam is thinking the same thing." The darkness didn't hide Aiden's grin.

But at least it hid Anna's blush.

"That was so much fun, Mom!" Cassie attached herself to Anna's side. "Can we play again?" A yawn punctuated the question. "Please?"

Anna didn't have to look at her watch to know it was way past the girls' bedtime. "It's getting late, Cass. Time to go home." She turned to Sunni before they could protest. "Thank you for inviting us to stay for dinner."

"Don't thank me." Sunni flashed a smile at Cassie and Chloe. "When you and the girls are here, Lily and I don't feel so outnumbered."

"Can we say good-night to the kittens, Mom?" Chloe pleaded.

Anna hesitated. Now that the adrenaline was wearing off, fatigue rolled in like fog and clouded her thinking. What other reason could there be for letting Liam get that close to her?

"Please?" Cassie joined the chorus. "Just for a minute?"

"Just for a minute," Anna agreed. "And when we get home it's a shower and straight to bed."

"Okay!" Cassie and Chloe darted toward Liam's workshop in case Anna changed her mind.

"Speaking of four-legged friends, I think I'll drive over to the shelter and check on one of our new arrivals," Sunni said. "He wasn't talking to me after the vet gave him a rabies shot this morning."

"I can do it." Aiden offered. "Liam can ride along and keep me company. We'll review the tape from tonight's loss, and I'll help him form a new strategy."

Liam shook his head. "I thought Brendan was the bossy one."

"I've been taking lessons." Aiden grinned at Anna. "After you, my lady."

Anna was grateful for Aiden's presence as they walked down the driveway. He cracked jokes with Liam and teased Anna constantly but she didn't take him seriously. Over the last few years she'd watched the youngest Kane brother charm every single woman between the ages of one and one hundred, whether he strolled down the aisle of New Life Fellowship or stood in line at The Happy Cow.

The girls appeared a few minutes later. They weren't moving as quickly now, a sign the day was finally catching up with them. Anna stowed their backpacks under the seat and helped them get settled before sliding into the driver's seat.

She turned the key in the ignition and winced when the van backfired and a puff of smoke erupted from the muffler. A mechanic had assured Anna the vehicle was safe to drive, so Anna had been saving to cover the cost of repairs.

Aiden's pickup idled a few yards away, and he waved his arm out the window, signaling her to go first. They followed her all the way to Castle Falls, and Anna exhaled a sigh of relief when the truck turned onto the road leading to the animal shelter.

Just as she'd expected, both girls were sound asleep by the time Anna pulled into the driveway. Rust sprinkled to the ground like confetti when she slid the back door open.

"Cassie. Chloe. We're home."

Cassie grunted something unintelligible, and Chloe stirred but didn't open her eyes.

Anna sighed. She hated to wake the girls, but at this point, other than letting them spend the night in the car, she didn't have a lot of options.

Headlights washed over her, illuminating the front yard. Instead of continuing down the street, the vehicle turned into the driveway and parked behind her.

Liam hopped out of the driver's side of Aiden's truck. Anna didn't see anyone else in the cab, which meant he'd left his brother at the shelter.

"Did I forget something?"

"No." He glanced at the girls sound asleep in the van. "I wanted to make sure you got home okay."

"So Aiden is checking on the shelter and you're checking on me."

"Right."

Anna mustered a smile. "I've been getting home okay with no one to check on me for years."

Liam didn't smile back. "Well, tonight you don't have to."

He didn't give Anna a chance to protest as he reached for Cassie and scooped her up in his arms. Anna followed him upstairs and sifted through the girls' pajama drawer while Liam went back for Chloe.

By the time he returned, both girls were awake, and neither one seemed the least bit surprised to see Liam there.

"I'm thirsty, Mom," Chloe murmured.

"I've got it." Liam ducked out of the room, and, a moment later, Anna heard the faucet running in the bathroom. She helped the girls into their nightgowns and was tucking them underneath the covers when Liam returned with two glasses of water. He handed one to Cassie and the other to Chloe.

It felt strange, having someone other than Anna's mother assist with the bedtime routine. The room seemed smaller than usual, the air sweetened by the evening breeze filtering through the window screen.

"Where's Clover, Mom?" Cassie sat up again, panic in her eyes.

"I'm sure he's here somewhere, sweetheart." Anna patted at the lumps in the comforter for the stuffed animal Cassie had had since birth.

"Green? One ear?" Liam held up the bunny. "Likes to hide under beds?"

Cassie grinned and hugged the toy against her chest.

"Lights out now, girls. It's way past your bedtime."

Chloe took a few sips of water and set the glass down on her nightstand. "Are you going to say prayers with us, Liam?"

"Sure." The bedspring squeaked as Liam sat down on the end of the bed.

Cassie started with the waffles they'd had for breakfast and worked her way through the day.

"God...thank You for the adoption-day party—"

"And firefly tag," Chloe whispered.

"And help Liam's kittens get adopted, too, because they need a good home. And bless Lily and Brendan and Sunni and Aiden and Mom and Liam."

Mom and Liam.

Panic drove a spike through Anna's heart. She pushed to her feet the moment Cassie and Chloe chimed an amen.

"Good night." She pressed a kiss against the top of their heads. "No talking now. We've got a busy day tomorrow."

The stairs creaked under Liam's weight as he followed her down the stairs.

Anna became aware of two things. The state of her living room and the frown etched between Liam's brows when he noticed the cardboard boxes strewn around the room.

"I'm sorry it looks so cluttered." Anna grabbed a throw pillow off the floor and tucked it in the corner of the couch where it belonged. "I'm not sure how, but my house ended up being reunion central. Courtney dropped off a box of decorations after church on Sunday and I haven't had a chance to go through them yet."

"I can help."

"No." Anna's voice came out sharper than she intended.

Her emotions were too close to the surface. Liam fit so so…*seamlessly*…into the fabric of their family. Anna was afraid the twins were getting too used to having him in their lives.

"It's late and—" *I'm afraid I'll get used to this, too.* "I have to call Courtney back."

For a moment, it looked like Liam was going to insist. But he nodded, instead.

"Good night, Anna."

She heard every creak in the ancient floorboards as he walked toward the door. It closed behind him, a soft click that echoed like a pistol blast in the quiet living room.

Anna's fingers dug into the back of sofa. Through the window, she watched the taillights of the pickup fade as it disappeared around the corner.

While she'd helped with the last-minute preparations for the party, Lily had told her it was Liam who'd contacted the rental company and set up everything.

He'd done nothing wrong, but Anna had resisted his help at every turn.

You lose people's respect when you can't stand on your own two feet, Anna, Ross had said. *It makes you look weak.*

He wouldn't let Anna ask anyone for help. Not even their parents. But it didn't prevent him from getting angry when Anna had a hard time keeping up the apartment after the twins were born.

He complained if the bills began to pile up on the counter or there were dishes in the sink.

Anna had learned to hide her fatigue behind a smile.

Learned to juggle a dozen different things in order to keep things running smoothly, but there were times she'd failed.

That's when Anna realized Ross had spoken the truth. But her husband's respect wasn't the only thing she'd lost. When Ross's dreams of a football career began to unravel and Anna couldn't fix it, he'd stopped loving her, too.

The times Ross had reached for Anna had left her bruised and shaken. She'd been shaken, too, when Liam's arms had come around her, absorbing the brunt of their fall.

Not only because Anna had never expected to feel safe in a man's arms again...but because she'd wanted to stay there.

"Does Anna know you stole her van yet?"

"Not yet." Liam rolled onto his side and grabbed a wrench from his toolbox. "And, if I recall, you were with me at the time. In fact, I think your exact words were, 'Grand theft auto? I'm in.' Are there any other misdemeanors or felonies on your bucket list I should know about?"

"None that I can think of at the moment."

"Good to know." His little brother. Such a kidder. "I did leave a note on Anna's door." The door she'd practically closed in his face the night before. "Lily is going to drop her off at work when she picks up the twins this morning. I'll have the van finished by the time her shift is done."

Liam tightened the bolt on the muffler he'd picked up at the auto-parts store. Frank, the head mechanic, attended Liam's men's group at church. The guy had been pestering Liam about organizing an overnight campout, so Liam used that as leverage to get him to open up a few hours early.

"I am curious about something, though," Aiden mused. "Is stealing a girl's car a creative way of letting her know you like her? If it is, your social skills in the dating department need an upgrade. Most guys start with dinner and a movie."

It was a moot point because Liam didn't date much. Okay, not at all. It was a choice he'd made. But if he ever did look for someone to share his life with, everything Liam wanted in a woman was… Anna.

He squinted up at his brother. "Is there a reason you're here?"

"While I was in the shower, Brendan left a text on my phone about a mandatory meeting.

Am I the only one in trouble, or did you receive a summons, too?"

"I got it." Liam's cell had chirped the announcement at six in the morning.

"Any idea what it's about?"

"Not a clue, but I hope it's another order." Because that would mean Liam had a good excuse to skip his class reunion on Saturday. "Mom mentioned Bren had gotten a bid from a camp in Minnesota, and I can smell cinnamon rolls. You know she only makes those for special occasions."

"Or comfort food."

"Do you have a guilty conscience or something?" Liam stood up and tucked the wrench in his back pocket.

"I'm not the one who stole someone's van out of their driveway last night." Aiden's phone vibrated, and he glanced at the screen. "The five-minute countdown begins. Let's get this over with."

Liam washed up in the shop, and they walked to the house together. The door to Brendan's office stood open, but Liam almost knocked out of habit, anyway.

"Come in."

Brendan stood at the window but he wasn't alone. Sunni and Lily were there, too, and one look at their faces told Liam he'd been called in for a business meeting all right. But it was *family* business.

"What's going on?" Aiden must have felt the tension in the room, too, but, like always, he deflected it with a joke. "Did you turn down another million-dollar deal?"

"It wasn't a million…" Brendan stopped. "Just grab a seat, bro."

"Great." Aiden drew out the word. "He wants us sitting down for this."

Liam glanced at Sunni. She offered a feeble smile, and even Lily, the other optimist in the family, looked a little nervous.

Which, truth be told, made Liam a little nervous, too.

He sat down.

"There's something I have to tell you." Brendan cleared his throat. "Something I should have told you a long time ago, I suppose, but there was nothing I could do and it seemed that some things were better left in the past."

"So that means you made a decision that affected all of us, but you didn't bother to mention it," Aiden said. "Again."

Liam knew exactly what decision Aiden was referring to, and judging from Brendan's creased forehead, their oldest brother did, too.

"I…" Brendan glanced at Lily and seemed to

draw strength from her reassuring nod. "Yes. I did."

"Just tell us, Bren," Liam said. "Whatever it is, we can handle it. The three musketeers, remember?"

Words Liam thought would encourage his brother had the opposite effect. Brendan flinched as if Liam had physically struck him.

"We aren't the three musketeers," Brendan said tightly. "There are...four of us."

"Four?" Liam echoed.

"We have a sister."

Chapter Thirteen

Shock kept Liam rooted in place, but Aiden's burst of laughter fractured the silence that had descended on the room.

"A *sister*?" he repeated. "I think we would have noticed one of those hanging around the house."

Brendan didn't join in, which made Aiden's reaction all the more jarring.

"Mom hid the pregnancy from us. She didn't want Dad to know because—" a muscle ticked in his jaw "—well, the baby might not have been his. It was after she'd filed for divorce."

Liam finally found his voice. "Mom *told* you that?"

"She didn't tell me anything. The only reason I found out about the baby was because I overheard her talking to a woman from the adoption agency. I'd skipped school and was keeping a low profile in our room so Mom didn't know I was there."

"How could she keep something like that a secret?" Aiden's voice thinned, a sign he was struggling for control. "Women gain weight when they're pregnant, right? I think we would have noticed."

Liam wasn't so sure. Their mom had never cared much about her appearance. Her wardrobe consisted of oversize T-shirts and sweatpants from the neighborhood thrift store. Clothing that would have made it easy to conceal a pregnancy from her sons.

"It wouldn't be as difficult as you might think." Lily spoke Liam's thoughts out loud. "Especially if your mom knew she wasn't planning to keep the baby."

Fragments of memories continued to piece themselves together in Liam's mind. His mom napping a lot. Yelling at them to be quiet because she didn't feel well. Carla was an alcoholic, though, so it wasn't as if that kind of behavior was out of character.

Sunni joined the conversation for the first time. "When Brendan asked if you could keep your last name while I was pursuing the adoption, I didn't question it. I assumed it was important to you boys to keep that small connection to your family."

Family? Liam hadn't known what the word meant until God had brought Sunni and Rich Mason into their lives.

Darren Kane had wandered in and out of their lives for years. No one knew how long he would stick around. Sometimes it was a few months, other times a few days. When he and Carla finally split up for good, Liam's mom had remarried and things had continued to go downhill from there.

The first few times Liam been placed in emergency foster care, Aiden and Brendan had been with him. But as they got older, it became more difficult to find someone willing to take in three boys who were already beginning to exhibit signs of the emotional wear and tear from growing up in such an unstable environment.

"*You're* our family." Liam reached for Sunni's hand and gave it a squeeze.

"Do you know where she is now?" Aiden rose to his feet. "Did she contact you?"

"No."

It wasn't the answer Aiden wanted to hear. "Well, what about the couple that adopted her? Do you know anything about them?"

Brendan shook his head. "It was a closed adoption. I remember Mom saying she didn't want any surprise visits down the road."

Closed. The word settled over the room with

the weight of a late-spring snowstorm, chilling the air around them.

"How old is she?" If possible, Aiden looked even more upset.

"You were around three at the time, so she would be in her midtwenties now."

She.

Every time someone said the word, it landed like a hammer strike on Liam's chest.

They didn't even know their sister's name.

"Why are you telling us this now?" Aiden took a restless lap around the room and stopped in front of Brendan, his hands clenched at his sides.

"To be honest…I'm not sure." Brendan's lips twisted. "But I've been praying about it and I've felt God telling me that it's time. And last night… watching Anna's twins tear around the yard…it reminded me there's a hole in our family."

"A hole you didn't bother to mention for over twenty years."

"Aiden—" Tears sparkled in Lily's eyes and she put a protective hand on Brendan's shoulder. "Brendan believed he was doing the right thing."

"We were kids. It wasn't like we could have done anything," Brendan said. "I was afraid if I told you…well, she would be one more person you'd…lost."

In other words, their big brother thought he'd been protecting them.

"I'll be back later." Aiden flung the words over his shoulder as he stalked toward the door.

"Aiden—"

"Let him go." Liam caught Brendan's arm as he started after their brother. "He'll work it out on the river."

Brendan blew out a sigh. "Why am I having second thoughts about telling you this?"

"Don't. It was the right thing to do." Even if the announcement was long overdue.

Liam understood Aiden's frustration. He was glad Brendan had finally confided in them, but what were they supposed to do with the information? Based on what Bren had said, their sister would be twenty-five years old. If she'd wanted to track down her biological family, wouldn't she have done so by now?

"I better get back to work." Although for a moment, Liam fought the temptation to grab a canoe and follow his younger brother.

Lily caught up to him at the front door.

"Anna called me a few minutes ago..." Lily paused, giving Liam time to confess.

"She found my note," he guessed. "Aiden and I followed her into town last night and I was afraid her van would break down on the side of the road. Before we came home, I...borrowed it and replaced the muffler and timing belt to prolong its life. The long-term prognosis isn't good, though."

A smile chased the shadows from Lily's eyes. "And I thought Aiden was the risk taker in the family. I'm heading over to her house now."

"Let Anna know I'll drop off the van after lunch so she can pick up the girls when she gets off work."

"I'm not watching Cassie and Chloe today. Anna decided to take the afternoon off. She said something about a prior commitment."

Uh-huh. A prior commitment, or was Anna upset he'd crossed a line and butted into her life again?

The weight on Liam's chest doubled in size.

"Then I guess I'll drop the van off and hope a sheriff's deputy isn't waiting to take me to jail."

"I'll post bail." Lily's eyes twinkled. "Some people may question your methods, but I have a feeling if you'd offered to fix Anna's van she would have said no. She's very independent."

Independent. Intelligent. A great mom. Beautiful.

Stubborn.

Liam had added that one to the list last night.

"Anna was that way in high school, too. She was always the one organizing activities and heading up fund-raisers for the athletic club. I don't know how she ended up with the highest

GPA in our class, because she helped out at the ice-cream shop on evenings and weekends."

"Some people are more comfortable giving than receiving."

Lily's voice dropped to a whisper. "And some people believe their value is based on what they do, not who they are."

Brendan. Lily knew his brother well. Liam silently thanked God for bringing the right woman into his life.

Although Sunni would no doubt take some of the credit for that, too.

"Now, I better scoot or Anna will be late for work." Lily grabbed her purse off the hook near the door.

Work. Right. But it was going to be difficult to concentrate after the bomb Brendan had just dropped.

Lily must have read his mind. "Liam?" She squeezed his arm. "Don't give up, okay?"

"I won't. Brendan might be a bossy control freak sometimes, but he's still my big brother."

Lily smiled.

"I was talking about Anna."

The gunmetal clouds mirrored Liam's mood as he walked back to the shop.

Give up on Anna?

It wasn't like you could give up on someone who'd never been yours to begin with.

A bright yellow envelope propped up on the work bench caught Liam's eye, but it was the rainbow of flower-shaped stickers covering the seal that made him smile.

Cassie and Chloe must have sneaked it inside when they'd said goodbye to the kittens the night before.

Liam slid his thumbnail underneath the flap and pulled out a handmade invitation. The Sunflowers were hosting a special banquet for friends and family at New Life Fellowship.

He glanced at the date.

Tomorrow night.

"Aren't you going to fix your hair, too, Mom?"

Anna straightened the bow at the end of Cassie's French braid and glanced at her reflection in the mirror. She wore her hair up in a ponytail—just like she did every day—and only a few stray wisps had managed to escape.

"I don't have time, sweetheart. The banquet starts in half an hour and I want to make sure Ms. Shapiro doesn't need help in the kitchen."

"But you *always* wear it like that," Chloe said.

Anna didn't know why her hairstyle was suddenly the focus of the twins' attention. "I'm not going to be part of the program, so I'm not the one who has to look pretty tonight. Now find your shoes and let's scoot."

The word *shoes* had the opposite effect on the girls. Because now they were frowning down at her feet.

"You should wear the ones you bought last summer," Cassie said.

"I'm not sure where they are..." Or if she'd even kept them. The shoes, delicate strips of bronze leather studded with multicolored beads, had stood out like a beacon amid the jumble of canvas slip-ons and flip-flops on an end-of-the-season clearance rack at the variety store. Anna had bought them on a whim. The heels were too high to be practical, more suited for a romantic date than dishing up ice-cream sundaes or mowing the lawn.

"I'll find them!" Chloe disappeared, and Cassie was already tugging the elastic band out of Anna's ponytail.

She decided it was easier to give in than fight her tomboy-turned-fashionista daughters' sudden urge to give their mother a makeover. At least they hadn't complained about what she was wearing...

"This will go way better with the shoes, Mom!" Chloe returned, sandals in hand, holding a strapless sundress Anna hadn't worn in years. She'd bought the emerald green chiffon for a friend's wedding, and it had been hanging

in the back of Anna's closet so long ago it had
come back in style.

"It's—"

"Perfect!" Cassie declared.

Ten minutes later, three inches taller, and
wishing she'd tossed on a cardigan, Anna followed the twins to the van.

The van with the new muffler that purred like
one of the kittens living in Liam's workshop.

Fortunately, Anna had spotted the note tucked
in her screen door before she'd noticed the empty
spot in the driveway.

Liam had stolen her van and…fixed it.

After keeping his distance over the past five
years, Liam Kane had scaled the invisible wall
they'd both known existed but had never for-
mally acknowledged. He had totally, undeniably,
invaded her life. And now he was invading Anna's thoughts…and, lately, her dreams.

But dreams are dangerous things.

Anna had told herself that for years. If she
didn't dream, she wouldn't be disappointed. *Or
disappoint someone else.* But for some reason,
the words lacked the power they'd once had.

"There's Grandma and Grandpa Leighton."
Cassie waved to Douglas and Barbara, who stood
waiting at the entrance of the church.

Anna had told her in-laws about the Sunflowers banquet, but she hadn't expected them to at-

tend. Barbara and Douglas had been in town during soccer season the summer before, but they'd politely turned down every invitation Anna had extended to watch the twins play.

"It's only a church-sponsored team, isn't it?" Douglas had asked.

Anna knew what her father-in-law was thinking. If a sport was for fun and not competition, what was the point? Ross had felt the same way. His identity had become so wrapped up in being an athlete that when Ross's behavior had put his football career in jeopardy, he'd started drinking, which had only made the situation worse. Barbara's lips closed as tight as the clasp on her designer handbag as Anna approached.

"I didn't realize the banquet was a formal affair." Her gaze swept over Anna. "I barely recognized you."

Anna barely recognized herself. She couldn't remember the last time she'd dressed up for a special occasion. And the hairstyle the girls had chosen wasn't really a style at all. They'd insisted Anna let her hair flow loose around her shoulders. But the disapproving look on Barbara's face made Anna wish she'd insisted on wearing the T-shirt dress and leggings she'd originally picked out for the event.

"Doesn't Mom look pretty, Grandma?" Cassie pointed to Anna's shoes.

"We picked out her dress, too."

Barbara's expression softened when she looked down at her granddaughters. "You two look adorable." She refrained from commenting on Anna's dress. "Your grandpa and I are looking forward to the program this evening."

Anna stepped aside to let a group of people pass and realized she still hadn't checked in with the Sunflowers leader.

"If you'll excuse me, I can meet you in the fellowship room in a few minutes," she told Barbara and Douglas. "Rene might need my help with some last-minute details."

Douglas inclined his head and ushered Barbara toward the doorway that led to a comfortable gathering room. The congregation had continued to grow after Seth Tamblin had accepted the call as pastor and the congregation had voted to build an addition the summer Anna returned to Castle Falls.

"Hurry, Mom!" Cassie urged. "We don't want to be late!"

"Hey, you were the ones who insisted I wear heels," Anna pointed out. "Now I know how Barbie feels."

"You're not Barbie, Mom," Cassie said. "You're a princess."

"Like Cinderella," Chloe agreed.

They linked their arms through Anna's in an

attempt to hold her steady. She took a wobbly step forward, felt her shoe snag in the Berber carpet and started laughing.

"Cinderella, it is. Because I have a feeling before the night is over I'm going to lose a shoe!"

Anna was still laughing when she rounded the corner at the end of the hall. And came face-to-face with Liam.

He wore gray slacks and a white button-down shirt that accentuated his striking blue eyes the way a snow-covered field complemented a January sky.

"I..." Anna couldn't think of anything else to say.

Fortunately Liam didn't seem to notice. He seemed at a loss for words, too.

Chapter Fourteen

Liam blinked. Twice. Just to make sure the woman standing in front of him wasn't a figment of his imagination.

Nope—Anna was still there.

Her hair, usually confined to a neat ponytail, flowed over her shoulders and she wore a dress that skimmed her slender curves and ended in a flirty ruffle at her knees. His gaze traveled a little farther, skimming over shapely suntanned legs and down to the pink toenails peeking out from the open tips of her beaded high heel shoes.

"Anna." His voice cracked like a twelve-year-old boy's on the cusp of puberty.

"Liam! You're here!" Cassie and Chloe released their hold on Anna and latched on to him instead.

"Of course I'm here." Liam dragged his gaze away from Anna and tweaked the ends of their copper braids. "I received an invitation to the ball, didn't I?"

"It's a *banquet*." Chloe giggled. "We're having barbecue chicken and mashed potatoes and green beans—but you don't *have* to eat those—and cake—"

"Josie's mom made it, so it prob'ly won't taste as good as the one we had for Mom's birthday," Cassie interrupted.

An image of Anna closing her eyes before she'd blown out the candle on her birthday cake downloaded in Liam's brain.

Anna didn't know he'd made a wish that day, too. He'd wished they didn't have the memory of prom night hanging over them like a shadow. He'd wished they could start over—that Anna would see him through new eyes—without the past getting in the way.

"Liam." Anna cast a quick look over her shoulder. "I—I didn't expect to see you here."

Liam had already figured that out. The startled expression on her face had been more than a reaction to almost colliding with him in the hallway. Anna hadn't expected to see him at all.

Now he knew why Cassie and Chloe had gone back into his workshop the night before. It hadn't only been to say good-night to the kittens. They'd wanted to personally drop off his invitation to the banquet.

Maybe they really were in cahoots with Sunni. And Lily. And his brothers.

"There you are, girls!" Rene Shapiro emerged from a doorway down the hall and spotted them. "We're going to line up for the opening song in a few minutes."

"Did you need help with anything?" Anna asked.

"Thank you, but it's all under control." Rene turned down the offer with a smile and ushered the twins away. "We'll see you inside."

A microphone crackled, cutting through the buzz of conversation inside the fellowship hall.

"I guess that's our signal," Liam said.

"Yes…" Anna glanced over her shoulder again.

Was she waiting for someone? Or was she reluctant to be seen in his company? Liam knew it didn't take much to grease the wheels of the small-town rumor mill.

A perky teenage girl Liam recognized from Seth's youth group blocked their entrance. "Hey, Anna! We have assigned seating this evening and you're at table six." She grinned at Liam. "You're wearing a boutonniere so you'll be at table one."

Liam glanced down at the gigantic silk sunflower another banquet volunteer had pinned to the front of his shirt when he'd arrived. The boutonniere was gaudy, but at least it didn't come with clown shoes and a tux.

The teenager abandoned Anna inside the fellowship hall and escorted Liam to a rectangular table covered in white paper directly in front of the stage.

Liam tried not to look at Anna as he took his seat, but he might as well have tried to stop his heart from taking its next beat.

He'd never seen her with her hair loose around her shoulders. And that dress…

Is stealing a girl's car your way of letting her know you like her? Because most guys start with dinner and a movie.

Aiden had no idea what he was talking about. Mr. Personality had no problem talking to women. Small talk had never come easily for Liam, but asking Anna out on a date…

"Chicken?"

Liam's head snapped up. "No—"

Not a chicken. A *realist*.

"Oh, come on. You have to try a piece. It smells delicious." The middle-aged woman sitting next to Liam passed a platter piled high with the main course.

"Thank you." Out of the corner of his eye Liam caught a flurry of movement as the teenage greeter helped seat two more people at Anna's table.

Douglas and Barbara Leighton.

Liam was suddenly glad he'd been placed at a table on the other side of the room. He couldn't imagine spending an entire evening with Ross's parents.

Rene Shapiro unhooked the microphone from its stand as the Sunflowers filed into the room and formed a line next to her. Cassie and Chloe ended up right in front of Liam, close enough that he could see the pins Anna had designed scattered along the necklines of their matching yellow vests.

"First of all, I would like to thank each and every one of you for attending our banquet. It's the Sunflowers' way of saying thank you to their friends and family, and they have a very special program planned for you this evening.

"Before we begin, however, I would like to take a moment and introduce everyone to our guests of honor." Rene focused her smile on Liam's table. "The Sunflowers wanted to recognize certain people who took time away from their busy schedules over the past few weeks and helped them complete one of their projects."

The conversation and clatter of silverware subsided as the spotlight bounced away from the Sunflowers' leader and landed on table one.

As it swept over the other guests, Liam realized everyone at his table wore a giant silk sunflower.

Suddenly, he had a very bad feeling about this…

"Lorraine Hutchins." Rene motioned for the woman to stand up. "Lorraine helped Audra Simmons earn her Lydia pin by sewing receiving blankets for a maternity home in Grand Rapids."

Lorraine waved and everyone applauded. Rene continued down the row, but Liam couldn't concentrate on what she was saying. The heat of the spotlight caused beads of sweat to pop out on his brow, but that was nothing compared to the animosity radiating from the table where Anna sat with Douglas and Barbara Leighton.

"Liam Kane."

Rene was looking at him expectantly and Liam realized it wasn't the first time she'd called his name. He rose to feet.

"Liam has been fostering a cat and her litter of kittens through our local animal shelter. He helped Cassie and Chloe Leighton design and construct a playground to keep the kittens busy until they're placed in permanent homes. The girls will be receiving their Caring for God's Creatures pin at our meeting next week."

Liam's tablemates smiled indulgently as he waved and sank back into the chair. The spotlight trailed across the floor and hovered over the row of Sunflowers again.

"I asked all the girls to share some of the memory verses they've been working on this week."

Rene nodded at the girls, and some of the bolder ones stepped closer to the microphone.

"'Are not two sparrows sold for a penny?'" Cassie's voice rose above the others, her voice clear and confident. "'Yet not one of them will fall to the ground apart from the will of your Father…'

"'And even the very hairs of your head are all numbered.'"

The others joined in and Liam silently recited the words with them. "'So don't be afraid. You are worth more than many sparrows.'"

Liam didn't dare look over his shoulder at Anna, so he focused his attention on the twins, instead. They beamed down at him as they recited the passage and Liam felt an unexpected surge of emotion.

Had his younger sister been given opportunities like Anna provided for Cassie and Chloe? Were her adoptive parents believers? Did she have blue eyes like Liam and his brothers?

Did she *know* she had brothers?

If Brendan had told them about their sister's existence years ago, they could have tried to find her. But now that so much time had passed, what if she assumed it meant they didn't want to?

Liam gripped the back of the chair to hold himself steady as the barrage of questions distilled into one.

Was she happy?

* * *

The moment Rene Shapiro announced Liam's name, the temperature in the air around Anna's table had grown colder than the waters of Lake Superior.

It reminded her of the evening they'd eaten together at Twin Pines. Cassie and Chloe had chattered on about Liam and the kittens and the project he'd supervised and Anna had felt the Leightons' disapproval then, too.

"I thought you said your friend was keeping an eye on my granddaughters," Douglas had said when the twins had gone over to the salad bar.

"Lily got tied up with a business call." Anna had struggled to maintain her smile. "I'm sure you understand what that's like."

Her father-in-law hadn't looked very understanding and Anna was relieved when he and Barbara decided to go straight home from the restaurant.

She'd been hoping the girls wouldn't bring up Liam's name at the banquet and they hadn't. They'd invited him to attend, instead!

"If my granddaughters needed help with something, I'm more than capable," Douglas had muttered after Rene motioned for Liam to stand. "All you had to do was ask."

It was difficult for Anna to imagine Ross's father putting up with a litter of kittens, let alone building a whimsical playground to keep them out of trouble.

Several times during the program Barbara had complained they weren't close enough to see the girls, but Anna knew what really bothered her was that Liam literally had a front-row seat.

Not that he'd looked comfortable there.

In spite of their good intentions, Cassie and Chloe had pushed Liam into the spotlight, a place he avoided whenever possible.

"I hope everyone enjoyed the evening." Rene raised her voice over the hum of conversation. "Before our regular meeting next Wednesday, the Sunflowers will divide into teams for a scavenger hunt at Silver Leaf Trail. The girls will need an adult chaperone, of course, and they suggested we invite everyone sitting at the head table to join us.

"If you choose to accept this mission, everyone who agrees to join us on the adventure will be presented with a special pin of your own, created by our own Anna Leighton."

The spontaneous burst of applause took Anna by surprise.

She glanced over at the head table just in time to see Liam slip out the exit door that led to the parking lot.

Had he heard Rene's last-minute announcement?

"Excuse me." Her chair scraped against the

floor as she stood up. "I should find out if Rene needs any help cleaning up."

"We're going to say our goodbyes to the girls, then."

Barbara hadn't expressed her opinion of Liam out loud, but it was evident in the frown that had settled between her perfectly shaped brows and stayed there throughout the course of the evening.

"Thank you for coming to the banquet." Anna pressed out a smile. "I know it meant a lot to Cassie and Chloe."

"We always enjoy spending time with our granddaughters."

Somehow, Douglas's words came out sounding like an accusation.

Anna resisted the urge to apologize again.

After the Leightons left, Rene caught Anna's eye from across the room, where she'd gathered all the Sunflowers in front of the stage. She held up her camera and mouthed the words, *Ten minutes*.

Anna nodded and slipped outside the door Liam had used to escape.

The sun had melted into the horizon, bathing the clouds in an apricot glow. Liam's truck was still in the parking lot so Anna walked around the building. Several families had drifted outside for some fresh air, but there was no sign of Liam.

She was about to give up and go back inside the church when a movement near the soccer field caught her attention. A familiar figure was leaning against one of the maple trees, face turned toward the setting sun. Liam's posture didn't exactly invite company, but Anna's feet had carried her to his side before her head had an opportunity to catch up.

"Liam?"

His broad shoulders stiffened and the guarded look Liam cast in her direction affirmed he'd chosen this solitary spot for a reason.

Now if only she could think of something to say.

"I...thank you for fixing my van."

"Thank you for not reporting it stolen."

"Not many car thieves leave a note." Anna drew courage from the smile that flickered in Liam's eyes. "Or bring it back in better condition than it was when they took it."

His shoulders relaxed in a shrug. "I changed the oil and the belts look good. You should be able to get a few more miles out of it."

He'd checked the engine, too. Car maintenance was one of those things that had slipped farther and farther down the list over the past few months. Liam wasn't the first man who'd told Anna the van needed a new muffler, but the fact he'd taken matters into his own hands and done something about it warmed her heart.

"If anything else goes wrong with it, give Frank over at Riverside Auto Body a call. He's one of those old-fashioned guys who still operates on the barter system...and his wife likes jewelry."

"That's good to know." Except that Anna didn't want to talk about Frank at the auto-body shop.

Liam detached from the tree, signaling an end to their conversation, but Anna was reluctant to let him go.

"Did you enjoy the program?"

The split second of silence that followed gave Anna her answer.

"I'm sorry, Liam." The words tumbled out. "The girls didn't mean to embarrass you."

"Embarrass me?"

Anna nodded at the gigantic sunflower drooping over the pocket of his shirt. "Singling you out at the banquet. Not telling you in advance what they had planned."

"The girls surprised me, Anna, but I wasn't embarrassed."

"You looked upset when you left the fellowship room..." *Oops.* Anna was glad the shadows hid the heat that crept into her cheeks. She'd all but admitted she'd been watching him.

Liam's sigh stirred the air the between them. "I was thinking about my sister."

Anna stared up at him, not sure she'd heard him correctly.

"I didn't know you had a sister."

"I didn't, either, until today. Brendan called a family meeting this morning and told us. Turns out, *he's* known about her for years."

The edge of bitterness in Liam's voice was something Anna had never heard before. She scraped up enough courage to ask,

"What happened?"

"According to Brendan, Mom hid her pregnancy and gave the baby up for adoption after she was born. He overheard her talking to someone from the adoption agency about it." Liam's hands rolled into fists at his sides. "Mom mentioned a closed adoption, and Brendan thinks it was handled through a private agency."

"Sunni didn't know about her, either?"

"She was as shocked as the rest of us." Liam shook his head. "Bren said he did it to protect us, but you'd think he would have learned his lesson about keeping secrets after the last time."

"The last time?" Anna repeated cautiously.

"Brendan was negotiating a major deal with a sporting-goods chain last summer and never said a word about it. The CEO of Extreme Adventures wanted to put our canoes in all their stores but only if Brendan agreed to remove our company logo. The worst part was, he almost agreed."

"What changed his mind?"

"God…and Lily. Brendan claimed he was protecting us then, too, but Aiden and Sunni and I… we all had a stake in the decision. I didn't care about losing the deal. I was more upset Brendan kept it a secret and put a heavier burden on himself instead of sharing it with us."

A secret.

The word cut deep. Anna knew all about keeping secrets.

"Why did Brendan decide to tell you now?"

"A nudge from God…and firefly tag with your girls. Watching them play made Brendan think about her…" Liam tipped his head toward the sky. Closed his eyes. "How crazy is it that I don't even know my sister's name?" He answered the question with a low laugh that couldn't disguise an undercurrent of pain. "When Cassie and Chloe recited that verse about God keeping His eye on the sparrows, all these questions started to run through my mind. What is she like? Did anyone tell her about us? Does she think we abandoned her?"

"You were a child, Liam." Anna's heart ached for him. "You didn't abandon her."

"Aiden doesn't see it that way. He took it pretty hard, but I…the first thing I felt was relief. I was *glad* she didn't have to go through what we did." Liam's throat convulsed. "What does that make me?"

Anna forgot about keeping her distance from Liam. Forgot about protecting her own heart when it ached in response to his pain.

She reached out and took Liam's hand.

"A good brother."

Chapter Fifteen

Cassie and Chloe were playing in the yard with Feathers and her kittens when Anna arrived to pick them up on Friday. Sunni waved to her from the picnic table and Lily's basset hound, camped in the shade underneath one of the benches, barked a greeting.

The stack of cardboard boxes tilted as Anna guided her van into the empty spot at the end of the driveway where Liam's truck was usually parked. For a man who supposedly spent most of his time in the workshop, Anna hadn't seen him since the banquet on Wednesday night.

She felt a stab of guilt, wondering if she was partially to blame. According to Lily, the entire family had been pitching in to get everything ready for the class reunion the next day.

"Hi, Mom!" Chloe, who'd been sprawled on her back in the grass, sat up to greet her. An oversize polo with the Castle Falls logo brushed the knees of her bright pink shorts. It looked exactly like the one Liam had worn the day he'd taken them out on the river.

"The girls were helping me give Missy a bath this morning," Sunni explained. "Chloe was in the splash zone so her T-shirt is hanging on the line to dry."

"Sunni found a home for two of the kittens!" Cassie vaulted to her feet. "She's the best matchmaker in Castle Falls."

Anna smiled. "I heard about that."

Strangely enough, Sunni's cheeks turned pink. "You did?"

"Uh-huh. And I think it's great the way you personally find homes for the animals at the shelter."

"Oh…yes. The shelter." Sunni reached down and gave Missy an affectionate pat. "Sit down for a minute and have a glass of lemonade, Anna. Lily had to run over to the post office and sign for a package, but she made me promise I would keep you here until she got back." She reached for the pitcher in the center of the table. "Leftovers from the party, so it might be a little tart."

Cassie and Chloe scampered off to round up one of the kittens who'd wandered toward the woods, and Anna slid into the bench across from

Sunni. "I'm sure it's delicious. Not many people take the time to make lemonade from scratch anymore."

"Only for special occasions," Sunni confessed. "Adoption Day is one of those, so I tend to pull out all the stops." She filled a glass and handed it to Anna. "I guess in a way I'm trying to make up for the all the birthdays parties my boys missed out on while they were growing up."

The raw pain in Liam's eyes when he'd talked about his family told Anna he and his brothers had missed out on more than birthday parties.

Still, Anna couldn't imagine not celebrating the day the twins were born. Not only did she host a party for Cassie and Chloe's friends, she also decorated The Happy Cow with balloons and offered all her customers a free scoop of frozen custard, to include them in the celebration.

"Do they talk about it much?" Anna asked cautiously. "The past?"

"No." Sunni's eyes clouded. "Over the years I've managed to piece together enough bits of information to know it wasn't good. Rich and I had prayed for children for years, but we never dreamed God would answer it the way He did.

"While we were waiting to be licensed for foster care, I read every parenting book I could get my hands on. But nothing prepared me for the reality of opening our home to three troubled boys everyone tried to convince us would *be* trouble.

"All of them were so different...and the files from their social worker didn't help at all. There was plenty of information about their background, but nothing told me what they *needed*. So I chucked everything and started watching Liam instead."

Anna's heart rose and fell with a little bump. "Liam?"

"He understood them," Sunni said simply. "Brendan's file from his previous school claimed he was a poor student, but Rich and I didn't know it was because he'd spent more time taking care of things at home than he did on his schoolwork.

"Liam started to ask Brendan for help and at first I was a little hurt, but then I realized tutoring Liam was actually forcing Brendan to hone his skills in math and English." The memory kindled a smile in Sunni's eyes. "Within a few months, his grades came up. Brendan's teachers were amazed, of course—one of them even suggested he was cheating—but I don't think Liam was surprised at all. He knew his brother was smart."

"*And* he knew Brendan wouldn't want to admit he couldn't do seventh grade math," Anna guessed.

"Exactly."

"What about Aiden?"

Inexplicably, Sunni's smile faded.

"Aiden was only ten when the boys moved to Castle Falls, so we thought he would have the easiest time adjusting to a new home. It turned out to be just the opposite.

"Brendan was a walking powder keg, but Aiden—he was a flame. Bright. Always in motion." Sunni's voice dropped to a murmur. "Unpredictable. He didn't sleep more than four or five hours a night because of the nightmares."

"Nightmares?"

"It was terrible. Aiden wouldn't tell us what they were about. I would bring him a glass of warm milk and read to him, but nothing seemed to help. One night I heard a noise in the backyard, and when I looked outside, he and Liam were tossing a football around—at midnight.

"I marched out there, ready to fuss at them because it was a school night, but Liam didn't give me a chance. He looked at me and said, "Aiden needs to move, Sunni.' So I let him." Sunni's lips tipped in a wry smile. "I *still* let him. That's why it's been so quiet around here lately. Aiden took off for a few days, but don't worry—he'll be back in time to help with your class reunion tomorrow."

In light of what Sunni had just told her about Liam's family, the reunion was the last thing on

Anna's mind. "It must have been difficult. Finding out they have a sister."

"Lily told you." The words slipped out with a sigh.

"Actually..." Anna wasn't sure why she was reluctant to reveal her source. "It was Liam."

Sunni's eyes rounded. "Liam?"

"After the Sunflowers banquet, but don't worry. I won't tell anyone."

"I know you won't." Sunni brushed Anna's comment aside with a swish of her hand. "I'm just surprised Liam mentioned it."

To you.

The unspoken words danced in the air. And Anna couldn't help but notice that Sunni didn't look surprised. *Delighted* would have been a more accurate description.

"I kind of pried it out of him," Anna admitted.

"Pri—" Sunni pressed her hand against her lips to cover a cough. "You'll have to tell me how you did that sometime. Liam may be quiet, like my Rich was, but that doesn't mean he doesn't feel things deeply.

"When the boys moved to Castle Falls, Liam preferred to spend time with Rich in the workshop. I knew I should have encouraged him to get involved in some of the extracurricular activities the school offered, but I tried to pay attention to what Liam needed—like he taught me to do with his brothers—and what he needed the most was a father."

Anna wasn't sure that any amount of effort on Liam's part would have made a difference when it came to making friends at school. She thought of all the times she'd heard her classmates talk *about* Liam instead of talking *to* him.

Ross, who'd been on the JV football team when Brendan and Les Atkins clashed on a daily basis, had bristled whenever Liam was around. Anna could have stood up for him, but Ross had had a possessive streak and she'd sensed it would only make things worse.

"Did you ever meet Liam's parents?"

"No." It was the first time since Anna knew Sunni that she saw a spark of anger in her eyes. "And as far as I'm concerned, Carla and Darren Kane didn't deserve the title. Most of the time, the boys fended for themselves. Rich and I had gone to Detroit on a short-term mission trip, and he met Brendan at the soup kitchen where we were serving. Brendan was stealing food from the pantry to feed his brothers."

The pieces of Liam's past created a picture much worse than Anna had ever imagined. Now she understood why Liam had said he was re-lieved their sister had been raised in another home.

"Brendan resisted our help at first. He'd been

taking care of his brothers so long it didn't feel right to let someone else step in and help." Sunni shook her head. "Brendan still struggles with it on occasion. In fact, we had a conversation on that topic last night.

"Carla Kane put Brendan's baby sister up for adoption and he had no control over it. In his mind, admitting they had a sister was admitting he'd failed his family. Liam and Aiden see the situation a bit differently, I think."

"Liam said Brendan only placed a heavier burden on himself," Anna murmured.

"He did," Sunni agreed. "And—" the word slipped out in a sigh "—it wouldn't be the first time."

"The contract with Extreme Adventures?" And now Sunni knew Liam had told Anna about that, too.

Sunni didn't appear upset by Anna's admission. "If Brendan had signed that contract, he would have lost sight of the reason why Rich started this business and… I think he might have lost Lily, too."

Anna couldn't hide her shock. From the outside, Lily and Brendan's romance was straight from a fairy tale. Every time she saw the couple, they could barely take their eyes off each other.

"What happened?" The words slipped out before Anna could stop them.

"Until last summer, I had no idea Brendan had spoken with Rich a few hours before he died," Sunni said. "My husband told Brendan to make sure he supported me so that I could finish what we'd started. Brendan had assumed Rich was talking about Castle Falls Outfitters, and, for years, he poured everything into making the business a success.

"When he told me about their conversation, I knew there'd been a terrible misunderstanding. Rich and I had filed the paperwork to legally adopt the boys and, yes, he wanted Brendan to support me, but it was to make sure we would be a family—even if he wasn't part of it this side of heaven." Tears welled up in Sunni's eyes. "But Brendan didn't realize that. He thought he had to earn my love, and the way to do that was by making Castle Falls Outfitters a success.

"It broke my heart when I realized the burden Brendan carried had shaped the way he saw himself…and the way he saw God. It's not only important that we know who we are, we need to know *whose* we are." Sunni's hand reached out and covered Anna's. "Our hearts can get weighted down with so many things. Grief. Anger. Secrets. And those things only get heavier when we insist on carrying them ourselves."

Secrets.

Anna was afraid to look at Sunni. Afraid she was no longer talking about Brendan.

"Heads up!"

Liam caught the football hurtling toward him a split second before it crashed into his sternum.

Brendan grinned. "I always thought you should have put those Jedi reflexes to good use back in high school."

Liam tucked the ball under his arm. "In order to play football in this town, our great-great-grandfather would have had to have broken ground for the first schoolhouse."

Brendan gave him a funny look, but Liam noticed he didn't deny it. "Lily wants to know if you're going to watch the parade with us."

"I'm planning on it, but I wanted to make sure everything is ready for the reunion. There won't be a lot of time between the two."

"Everything will be ready if Courtney Meade doesn't drop off another truckload of stuff." Brendan sauntered over and pulled a catcher's mitt from one of the oversize plastic bins lined up in front of the lattice screen Liam had put up the day before. "What is all this, anyway?"

"Props for a photo booth. It was Courtney's idea. She thought it would be fun to recreate some of our high school highlights based on old photos she found in the yearbook."

"That doesn't sound like fun to me." Brendan tossed the catcher's mitt back in the bin. "If it was my reunion, forget the props. The student council would have to recreate the principal's office."

Liam snorted. "You wanted to hang out with Mr. Braeburn. He was on the board of directors for Camp While-Away, and they were in the process of expanding their waterfront activities. The canoes they ordered kept us out of the red that winter."

Brendan's eyes narrowed. "How did you *know* that?"

"I pay attention." Liam tossed the football in the air and caught it again. "You were already channeling your inner CEO at that age."

"Sunni thought the same thing, but without Rich, I was totally flying blind," Brendan admitted. "And I couldn't have turned Castle Falls Outfitters around without you. Don't ever think I took your sacrifice lightly."

The statement blew Liam away. "What sacrifice?"

"The chance to go to college. To live your dream instead of mine."

"But…what else would I have done?"

Brendan's response was a solid, brotherly punch to Liam's arm. "Are you kidding? You could have taken your mad design skills and earned a degree in architecture or civil engineering. You have a gift, Liam. Why do you think Rich let you hang around the shop and watch him for hours? He saw it, too."

Pursuing a career in those fields had never occurred to Liam. But a gift? That was a stretch. All Liam knew was that he loved watching a canoe take shape beneath his hands. To start with raw ingredients and make something that would help a person get up close and personal with nature. And, in the process, bring them closer to the One who'd created it.

"This is my dream." Liam hadn't said the words out loud before but knew it was true. "I wouldn't have stayed in Castle Falls otherwise."

"No regrets?"

Brendan's question grabbed hold of Liam's heart and squeezed.

"I wouldn't go that far," Liam muttered. "But we don't get a do-over."

"Sometimes we get a second chance, though." Brendan regarded him thoughtfully. "Lily gave me one."

Liam didn't like where this was going. "That's different.

"Lily didn't know anything about our family when she moved to town. She didn't look at you and see one of *those Kane brothers*."

His brother flashed a grin. "That was a pretty good impression of Mrs. Sedowski."

"It should be. I heard her say it often enough." Marge Sedowski had served on several of the committees Sunni had chaired over the years. She was also president of the Castle Falls Historical Society and could trace people's families back to the late 1800s. Based on the town archives, she knew who belonged in Castle Falls and who was an impostor. "Every time I run into her at the grocery store, she still looks at me like I'm twelve years old."

"That's probably because Mrs. Sedowski *is* seeing a twelve-year-old kid. The woman hasn't updated her glasses since the eighties."

Liam battled a smile and lost. "It doesn't change the fact that people have long memories."

"Not all the memories are bad."

Who *was* this guy? And what had he done with Liam's big brother?

"I know that," Liam said slowly. "But you and Lily…you started with a clean slate. She *chose* you."

And Anna had chosen Ross Leighton.

Chapter Sixteen

"I can't decide…" The customer—a man close to Anna's age who'd wandered into The Happy Cow—studied the board on the wall behind the counter with the same intensity and focus Anna had used to memorize the periodic table in eighth grade. "What would you recommend?"

Recommend?

Anna would recommend making a decision before the *next* Fourth of July rolled around—but that probably wasn't the way to encourage repeat business.

"A lot of my customers are ordering Fireworks today," she said, instead. "Chocolate-covered blueberries and fresh strawberries swirled into our homemade vanilla ice cream. Would you like to try it?"

"Your customers?" Interest sparked in the man's eyes. "You own this place?"

"Yes." Anna glanced out the window. Over the past few hours, a row of colorful lawn chairs had sprouted like wildflowers along the curb in front of The Happy Cow as people staked their claims along the parade route.

Nancy Foster had made a pact with the business owners on Riverside years ago that they would all remain open during the parade, a tradition Anna had continued when she took over. The chimes above the door had been jingling nonstop since she'd unlocked the door at nine o'clock that morning, a sound Anna was sure she was going to hear in her sleep for the rest of the summer.

But it wasn't her customers' fault she stood behind the counter, holding an ice-cream scoop instead of a camera.

Where are you, Chad?

Anna's teenage employee was scheduled to cover the parade and afternoon shift, but he hadn't shown up yet. Chad was a hard worker who could never quite make it to work on time. He would sit in his car, talking on the phone with his girlfriend until Anna tapped on the window to get his attention. But the main street was blocked off for the parade, and there was no sign of Chad or his car.

The customer's cell phone pinged, and he

winked at Anna as he unclipped it from a holder on his leather belt and glanced at the screen.

Anna took advantage of the moment to sneak a discreet glance at her own phone, hoping to see an I'm-on-my-way text from Chad. No new messages or missed calls.

Panic began to override Anna's initial frustration. She wasn't sure who she could find to take Chad's shift at the last minute. The majority of her employees were either in the parade or watching it with their friends and family.

Anna had dropped Cassie and Chloe off near the pavilion a few hours ago. Pastor Seth had encouraged the kids clubs at New Life Fellowship to enter floats in the parade, and Anna had promised the twins she would be cheering on the Sunflowers from the sidewalk…and taking pictures for their journals.

Her customer chuckled and slipped the phone back into its case. "Sorry about that. A doctor is always on call." His gaze drifted from the whiteboard to the collection of porcelain cows that grazed on a shelf near the cash register.

"Have you decided yet?" Anna resisted the urge to thump the ice-cream scoop against the counter like a gavel to keep him on task.

"I guess I'll try the Fireworks—" A wink *and* an eyebrow wiggle. "I like to live on the edge."

Oh, please.

Over the years, Anna had discovered there were two kinds of tourists. The ones who experienced the beauty of God's creation and the ones who admired it from the driver's seat of their convertibles.

From the expensive designer sunglasses propped up on the crest of his gelled hair to the Top-Siders that looked like he'd put them on straight from the box, Anna guessed her customer fell into the second category.

She couldn't help but compare him to Liam, whose jeans wore a velvety soft patina from *living*, not because they'd been manufactured to look that way.

"This is a nice place." The guy rested a hip against the stool at the counter and scanned the dining area. "A buddy and I invested in a restaurant last year. Improv. It was voted Best New Restaurant in the April issue of *Midwest Experience*. Have you heard of it?"

Liam didn't feel the need to list his accomplishments, either, although the fleet of canoes outside his workshop certainly gave him license to boast about his success.

"I'm sorry…but no, I haven't." Anna watched a little girl skip past the window, holding tight to the string of a star-shaped helium balloon. Her parents followed a few steps behind, scanning the curb for a place to sit down. Now the hedge of chairs was two deep as volunteer deputies ushered last-minute arrivals off the street.

"I suppose news still travels by telegraph way up here?" He laughed at his own joke. "If you're ever in Chicago you'll have to stop in and say hello. I'm Dawson by the way—" He reached across the counter and Anna handed him the cone.

"It's nice to meet you. That will be three dollars." The opening notes of "America the Beautiful" drifted through the open windows. The high school marching band always led the procession through town, blasting out a mix of patriotic tunes to remind the people lining the curb why they had gathered together. In a matter of minutes, they'd be turning the corner onto Riverside.

Anna resigned herself to watching the parade from the doorway. The number of parade watchers would hinder any attempt to get some good pictures, but at least she could wave to Cassie and Chloe when the Sunflowers' float went past.

"Keep the change." Dawson gave Anna a five-dollar bill.

"Thank you." She tucked the money in the cash register. "Enjoy the weekend."

"I will. I'm meeting up with some guys at their condo for the weekend. They weren't kidding when they said the scenery around here was beautiful…" Wink-wink. Maybe Dawson suffered from a permanent twitch. He gave Anna a moment to dive over the counter into his arms. When she didn't, he raised the cone in a friendly salute and strolled toward the door.

Liam was holding it open for him.

Liam. Here. And ruggedly handsome, even with a scowl on his face.

Definitely no comparison between the two men.

"Was that guy bothering you?" Liam demanded when the door snapped shut.

"No." Anna blinked. "Why?"

"Your cheeks are pink."

If her cheeks were pink, it was because of *him*.

A good-looking doctor from Chicago had left her cold while Liam raised the temperature in the air simply by walking into the room.

"Why are you still here?" He covered the distance between them in three strides.

"I'm working." One of the volunteer firefighters hit the siren and the piercing blast rattled the glass sundae cups lining the shelf behind Anna's head. "Why are *you* here?"

"Lily sent me to find you." Liam notched his voice above the cheer that rose from the pint-size members of the crowd outside when penny candy rained down from the ladder truck and pelted the sidewalk. "My family has a lawn chair reserved for you under the awning by the hardware store. You can't get prime frontage like that everywhere. It's a perk the president of the animal shelter gets for buying kibble in bulk."

In spite of the anxious knot that had formed in the pit of her stomach, Anna smiled. "I can't leave until Chad gets here. He's in charge of the next shift."

"When is it scheduled to start?"

"Twenty minutes ago."

"Why can't you put a Be Back Soon sign in the window and lock the door for an hour? How many people are going to want an ice-cream cone once the parade starts?"

"Not very many, but they expect the ice-cream shop will be open if they do," Anna said. "Do you want something?"

"Yes…I want you to go to the parade."

Before Anna could respond, Liam breached the narrow space between the counter and the cash register. A space that had always felt…spacious…until now.

"Go."

"Liam, no. I can watch the parade from the window."

"Or you can let me help you. I know the difference between Mackinaw Island Fudge and Moose Tracks. They have different labels. And if you're worried about me stealing money from the tip jar, let me assure you that I only steal cars."

Her gaze tangled with Liam's. He was staring

down at her with a mixture of exasperation and tenderness, but it was the tenderness that proved to be her undoing.

Forty-eight hours ago, Anna would have shooed Liam out the door with a smile. She could handle this on her own, thank you very much.

But that was before her conversation with Sunni Mason.

It had shed a light in the darkest corners of Anna's heart and shown her that she'd fallen into believing the same lie Brendan had. That her worth—in God's eyes and in the eyes of others—was based on what she accomplished, not on who she was. In her marriage, that had certainly been the case. When Anna had done things "right," Ross had been happy. If she hadn't, he'd blamed and belittled her until things got so turned around, Anna had begun to accept the lie as truth. And, like a weed, that one lie had sent out runners that had slowly captured more ground.

Asking for help meant weakness. If you trusted your heart to someone else's keeping, you gave them the power to break it.

Or heal it.

Another truth that sailed in on a fresh wind, only this time, instead of fighting the feeling that she was losing control, Anna leaned into it.

"All right."

"I can smile and count change…" Liam

stopped. And then, cautiously, he said, "What did you say?"

"I said all right. You can help me." Buoyed by the laughter welling up inside of her, Anna came up on her toes and slipped her arms around Liam's lean waist. "Thank you."

The hug was spontaneous. The kind Anna would have given a friend. But those kinds of hugs didn't blaze a path all the way down to her toes or rob her of the ability to speak.

Liam's arms tightened around her until the space between them slowly disappeared. Anna felt the rapid tempo of his heart. Saw his velvet blue eyes darken to indigo right before he bent his head and captured her lips in a kiss that made everything in the room fade away.

The kiss was unexpected and sweet, and Anna leaned into that, too.

She'd always wondered if she would ever feel safe in a man's arms again. But in Liam's embrace she didn't feel trapped. She felt…free.

And then, suddenly, she was.

Liam stepped away from her, his hands clenched at his sides.

"Anna…" Her name funneled out in a sigh. "I'm—"

The bells above the door clashed together in a series of off-key notes instead of their familiar, welcoming jingle.

Anna turned toward the sound, expecting to see Chad lope through the door, and found herself on the receiving end of her father-in-law's piercing glare.

Liam felt Anna stiffen beside him, but she didn't say a word as Douglas Leighton strode into The Happy Cow, blotting out the sun streaming through the window like an eclipse.

He wasn't sure if Ross's father had seen Anna in Liam's arms, but the fact they were breathing the same air provided enough evidence to judge them guilty.

"Mr. Leighton." Liam scraped up the manners Sunni had taught him, but Ross's father didn't bother to acknowledge him at all.

Seriously? Liam found it a little insulting to know he wasn't even worthy of the energy it required for Douglas to turn that disapproving scowl in his direction.

"Douglas." Anna's gaze bounced from Liam to Douglas and then back again. "I didn't expect to see you here. Barbara mentioned you'd be visiting friends over this weekend."

"We wanted it to be a surprise," Douglas said stiffly. "Barbara asked me to find you. Lyle Wilford invited us to join him and his wife for the parade."

Liam could tell Anna had no desire to sit in an

air-conditioned office on the second floor of the bank, sealed off from the laughter and the music, but she managed to produce a smile.

"I promised Cassie and Chloe I would take pictures of the Sunflowers' float when it went by."

"And you'll miss it if you don't go," Liam reminded her.

As if on cue, the first vehicle in New Life Fellowships flotilla—an ancient VW bus used to transport the youth group to various activities—rumbled past the window.

"Thank you. For—" Anna paused and a delicate rose blush worked its way into her cheeks "—taking over. Chad should be here any minute, though…"

"If he's not, don't worry." Aware that Douglas was blatantly eavesdropping on their conversation, Liam resisted the urge to give Anna a gentle nudge toward the door. "I've got this."

Douglas didn't follow Anna to the door. He waited until she was safely out of Liam's clutches before he exited the building.

Five minutes later, a lanky teenage boy hurtled through the door like he was being chased by a pack of wolves. He skidded across the freshly waxed floor, lost his balance and almost landed in a heap at Liam's feet.

"Chad?" Liam guessed.

"Uh-huh. I'm late…is Ms. Anna here? Is she mad I'm late?" The kid's hazel eyes expanded to the size of his Harry Potter frames as another, more terrifying thought, occurred to him. "Did she hire *you* to take my place?"

"Your job is safe—for now. But if I were you, I'd make sure 'Ms. Anna' can see her reflection in the floor when she gets back."

"Okay." Chad grabbed a clean apron from a hook behind the cash register. "I was with Erica—my girlfriend—" The panic dissipated, replaced by a goofy grin that exposed two gleaming rows of braces on his teeth. "And I forgot I was supposed to come in an hour early today, you know?"

Oh, Liam knew all right. He had a tendency to forget everything when Anna was nearby, too.

Like common sense. And self-control.

Liam suppressed a groan. Anna would probably lump him into the same category as the customer he'd caught flirting with her. At least Mr. Hair Gel hadn't crossed a line.

He could only imagine what was going through Anna's mind right now. She'd offered a simple gesture of appreciation and Liam had completely lost his head.

"Look out!" Chad had moved a plastic tray and inadvertently started a chain reaction that involved a donation can for the animal shelter and a glass filled with drinking straws. Liam managed to grab the straws before they flowed over the side of the counter.

"Is there anything I can do to help?" Chad might be one of Anna's employees, but, given his present state of mind, Liam wasn't convinced Chad would remember anything he'd been taught.

"Nope…" In his haste to chase down the last of the runaway straws, Chad tripped over a large cardboard box jutting out from the underneath the counter.

Liam heard a muffled clink as the contents shifted. "Let me get that out of your way." He picked up the box and saw the words *Anna's Inspiration* printed in large block letters above The Happy Cow's address on the shipping label.

"That goes upstairs." Chad peered over Liam's shoulder.

"It's probably jewelry stuff." He reached for the box, but Liam backed up a step.

Liam had a mental picture of Chad—and the box—tumbling down the stairs.

"I'll take it up there." The floorboards creaked under Liam's weight as he climbed the narrow staircase to the second floor. At the top of the stairs, the hallway branched off in two directions. Liam veered toward the doorway with a filmy curtain stretched across the opening.

He swept it aside, took a step and almost dropped the box.

Other than the seasonal flavors Anna added to the menu, The Happy Cow hadn't changed in years. In honor of its namesake—a smiling Holstein featured on the ads Anna placed in the weekly newspaper—the brick storefront was painted white with gigantic black polka dots. Lily would have called it creative marketing because the building drew more attention than a billboard on the highway. Inside, the decor could only be described as whimsical. A maze of wrought-iron bistro tables and chairs were spray-painted in a rainbow of colors. Wooden signs with cute sayings like Keep Calm and Add Sprinkles were plastered on the walls like bumper stickers.

Anna's studio evoked an entirely different feeling. The mellowed hardwood floors were original to the building, the walls were exposed brick—softly weathered charcoal grays and deep cranberry reds, not a single black polka dot to be seen. Edison lights in various lengths hung from the tin-punched ceiling like a cluster of wind chimes. Red Wing crocks filled with birch branches had been placed strategically around the room, but they were more than decorations. Anna used them to display her jewelry.

Liam took a slow lap around the room, amazed at her talent all over again. It was clear that what inspired Anna was the same thing that inspired him. A love for God's creation. Rings made from hammered copper filled ceramic bowls. There were wood violets carefully preserved in glass pendants, the delicate clasps on each one made to look like a tiny gold acorn.

Liam carried the box over to a table made of driftwood near the window. A variety of beads and bits of translucent glass filled ceramic containers. Some of them had already been strung on a slender piece of wire, along with—Liam bent down for a better look—a tiny charm that looked just like the tree Sunni had designed for the Castle Falls logo.

And that's when he saw it. Not a pattern, but a string of *moments*.

The colors Anna had chosen were the changing blues of the river, interspersed with bits of silver-green glass that represented the trees. A burgundy agate—*the campfire*?—and a chunky gray stone Liam guessed represented Eagle Rock.

A smile broke out across Liam's face.

If Anna wanted to remember their day on the river, maybe other people would, too.

And Liam had a hunch that Lily, the Castle Falls Outfitters enthusiastic marketing director, would feel the same way.

Chapter Seventeen

"Where's Liam, Mom?" Cassie hopped up on the curb and searched the faces of the dwindling crowd as they walked toward the van. "He said he'd be at the parade."

"I haven't seen him, sweetheart."

Not since Anna had left him in charge of The Happy Cow.

Not since he'd *kissed* her.

Anna still couldn't believe he'd kissed her.

But, then, she couldn't believe she'd practically thrown herself into his arms first.

Heat climbed into Anna's cheeks as she remembered how abruptly Liam had broken off the kiss.

"Anna...I'm—"

She'd had no idea what he'd been about to say when Douglas interrupted them.

I'm sorry? Disappointed in you?

"Mom?" Anna felt a tug on her arm. "I'm thirsty."

"We'll be home in a few minutes, sweetheart. Can you wait until then? I told Bethany to meet us there after the parade."

"Why can't we go to the reunion, too?" Cassie asked. "We won't get in the way, will we, Chloe?"

Chloe shook her head. "Promise."

"And I promise you'll have more fun with Bethany." Anna unlocked the van and opened the door. "Don't let the balloons escape." The entire back of the vehicle was filled with balloon bouquets Courtney had ordered from the Petal Pushers flower shop.

Over the last twenty-four hours, Anna had discovered her committee member had gone rogue and rented a photo booth, too. She wasn't sure what other surprises Courtney had in store for the afternoon.

On the drive home, the twins entertained Anna with stories of everything that had happened prior to and during the parade.

"Lily made a sign for us," Cassie said. "Did you see it, Mom?"

"It was difficult to miss." Even from the second floor of the bank. Although Anna had politely declined Douglas's invitation, she'd somehow ended up joining them anyway, sealed off from the people camped out along the curb.

With Rene's help, the Sunflowers had transformed a flatbed truck into a garden. On a crisp white bedsheet, their leader had painted Ready, Set, Grow!

Good advice for little girls…and maybe their mother, too.

Anna parked in front of the garage and the twins jumped out. She'd expected to see Bethany's bicycle propped against the porch rail, but it was nowhere in sight. Anna hoped that meant the teenager had decided to walk over. One employee showing up late for their shift was enough for the day. The reunion would be starting in an hour, and Anna still had a few last-minute details to take care of. Like finding places for the four dozen balloon bouquets crowding the back of the van.

The front door swung open, and Cassie let out a loud whoop.

"Grandi!"

Both girls charged across the lawn and threw their arms around Anna's mother.

"Surprise!" Laughing, Nancy Foster knelt down and pulled her granddaughters into a tight hug. "Look at you! You've both grown six inches since the last time I saw you."

"Mom." Tears stung Anna's eyes. "When did you get here? Why didn't you tell me you were on your way home?"

"Because it wouldn't have been a surprise!"

Another woman stepped onto the porch, a petite, silver-haired version of Anna's mother.

"Gram?" Anna choked.

Her grandmother grinned. "You weren't expecting to see me, were you?"

That was an understatement. Gram hadn't been home for a visit since she'd moved to Florida three years ago.

"I can't believe this." Anna's gaze shifted from Gram to her mom again. "The last time we talked, you said Gram wasn't doing very well."

"Did I?" Nancy leveled a meaningful look at Gram. "I must have been referring to her patience. Your grandmother wasn't following Dr. Hayward's orders to rest."

"Humph." Gram tossed her head. "Dr. Hayward doesn't know how quickly the Foster women heal." To prove her point, she ignored the railing and marched down the steps. When she got to the bottom, she opened her arms wide. "Well, do my two favorite girls have any hugs left for me?"

Cassie and Chloe flew to their great-grandmother's side, eager to oblige.

"We were in the parade," Cassie told her. "All the Sunflowers were."

"We helped Ms. Shapiro decorate the float, too!"

"It sounds like you've been busy." Nancy

slipped her arm around Anna's waist. "And speaking of busy...aren't you supposed to be at your class reunion?"

"It starts in an hour. I have to stop by work and grab a few things for the ice-cream-sundae bar before I head over to Sunni's."

"Sunni's?" Nancy repeated. "I thought you reserved the pavilion for the reunion."

"It's a long story. We had to switch venues at the last minute and Lily Kane came to our rescue. Castle Falls Outfitters is hosting it."

"Miss Lily has been watching us while Mom's at work, too," Cassie said. "And they've got kittens!"

"We helped—"

"Girls." Anna broke one of her own house rules and interrupted before the twins mentioned Liam's name. "Why don't you run inside and get a drink of water while I call Bethany? She should have been here by now."

"Oh, she was here, but I sent her home." Anna's mom didn't look the least bit repentant. "I haven't seen my granddaughters for months, and we have a lot of catching up to do."

"Lots of catching up!" Cassie echoed.

"That would be great." Anna was still trying to adjust to the fact her Mom and Gram were here. "I'm sorry I don't have time to catch up with you, too—"

"We'll have plenty of time tomorrow after church," Nancy said. "Don't worry about a thing. Gram and I will take the girls to the corn roast at the pavilion for lunch, and then she wants to take a peek at your studio, if you don't mind."

"Not at all." Anna hoped they wouldn't be disappointed.

Before she'd taken over The Happy Cow, Gram and her mom had talked about converting the upstairs into an extra dining room and adding a grill so they could expand the menu. Anna would have done it…if Lily hadn't fanned the flame of her dream and suggested she turn the space into a studio, instead.

"Now you better scoot. And don't worry about a curfew," Nancy teased. "I'll tuck the girls into bed if you want to watch the fireworks with your friends. I know you haven't seen some of them for years."

There was only one person Anna wanted to watch the fireworks with—and suddenly she wasn't sure he would even be at the reunion.

"That's it. You are officially off duty. Time to have some fun and let us take over." Lily tugged the clipboard out of Liam's hands. "This is your class reunion, you know."

Liam was fine right where he was, supervising the waterfront activities. Far from the tent where his classmates—and Anna—were reminiscing about the past.

She'd been one of the last of the committee members to arrive, and Liam couldn't help but wonder if he was to blame.

Of course you are. Idiot.

Liam could still feel Anna's slender arms around his waist.

She'd offered a simple gesture of appreciation and he'd turned it into something more.

But that was the problem. When it came to Anna, Liam *did* want more. He wanted the whole package. Wife. Children. The house with a picket fence. Or, in his case, a cabin in the woods.

"I have to stay here," Liam told his sister-in-law. "Someone might want to take out a canoe."

"In case you haven't noticed, the sun is starting to set," Lily said. "You already missed the root-beer floats, volleyball and a cutthroat game of horseshoes."

"And, in case you haven't noticed, Brendan's bossiness is rubbing off on you."

"I prefer to use the term *assertive.*" Lily grinned. "And, by the way, I told Brendan your idea about carrying a line of Anna's jewelry in the trading post, and he loved it. Have you told her yet?"

"It might be better coming from you."

Lily's eyes narrowed. "And why is that?"

"She might think I'm overstepping." Liam had already been guilty of that once today.

Idiot.

"Come on, everyone!" Courtney Meade had commandeered the microphone again. "Gather round! We have one more special activity, and then we'll caravan over to the boat landing to watch the fireworks."

Courtney's last "special activity" was forcing everyone to pose for the photo booth. Fortunately, Liam had managed to avoid that, too. While the rest of his classmates squeezed into old jerseys and posed for the camera, Liam had restocked all the coolers with ice.

"Liam—"

"I'm going. I'm going." And if he walked *really* slowly, maybe everyone would be leaving by the time he reached the tent.

No such luck. Courtney spotted him walking up the bank and waited for him to join the group. For the first time in ten years.

Liam's gaze slid to Anna. She'd changed clothes between the parade and the reunion, exchanging her knee-length denim skirt and white polo for the sundress that accentuated her slender curves.

"Still mooning over Anna, huh?" Eddie Norton, one of Ross's friends, wedged himself between Liam and the tent pole. "Some things never change."

Liam ignored him. The reunion was alcohol free, but that hadn't stopped some of the guys from smuggling in their own supply of beer. Eddie and his friends had grown increasingly louder and more obnoxious as the day went on.

"Ross didn't like you," Eddie said as pleasantly as if they'd been discussing the weather. "He was afraid Anna would break up with him and go out with you when he left for college."

Now Liam knew Eddie was drunk. Anna hadn't known Liam even existed in high school, and she certainly hadn't been interested in dating him.

"If I could have everyone's attention please…" Courtney glowered at Eddie. "I put together a video highlighting some of our favorite high school memories." She tapped a key on her laptop and a photo of the high school appeared on the side of the tent, as large as a movie screen.

A familiar song began to play in the background, and Liam realized it was the theme from their senior prom.

His stomach turned a slow cartwheel, and he glanced at Anna. She was staring up at the giant makeshift screen, her face pale.

Liam took a step toward her, but everyone pressed closer for a better view, hemming him in.

The video opened with a tour of the building. Courtney took them through the science lab and the library and then to the cafeteria, where Liam's classmates were gathered at tables based on their standing in the high school hierarchy.

Liam hadn't even eaten in the cafeteria. He'd sneaked outside and hung out with Brendan every day to make sure *he* ate lunch.

Courtney had done her homework. She'd found old photographs of the gymnasium and the football field. There was a close-up of Anna cheering at the top of the pyramid during a homecoming game and another shot of her playing the lead in the school play.

By the time Liam saw the gym decorated for their senior prom, he wanted to grab Courtney's laptop and toss it in the river.

He didn't care that he wasn't in any of the photos, but Anna…she was in almost every single one. And so was Ross.

The video ended with pictures of their high school graduation. Anna, the class valedictorian, stood at the podium, giving her commencement speech.

If this was hard on him, it had to be killing Anna.

Liam looked over at the place where she'd been standing.

She was gone.

Chapter Eighteen

Anna sank down to the ground and closed her eyes, but it didn't shut out the images rolling through her mind.

The video…it had felt like she was watching someone else's life.

If only she'd known what Courtney had planned…

You could have what? Pretended everything was okay? Pretended that Ross had whisked you away and you'd lived the storybook romance every girl dreams of?

She'd been doing that for years.

Anna had been protecting Ross's reputation in the eyes of his hometown. Protecting his memory so the twins would grow up never knowing Ross hadn't wanted to be a father.

Protecting herself from making a mistake in judgment again.

A tear slid down Anna's cheek, and she swiped it away with the back of her hand.

Sunni was right. It was a burden too heavy to carry alone.

I want to start over, Lord. I want to walk in freedom, not weighed down by the past.

A stick snapped a few feet away and someone emerged from the shadows.

She should have known Liam would seek her out.

He sank down onto the ground next to her. "I take it you didn't know about that part of the program."

Anna shook her head and then realized Liam couldn't see her in the dark. "No, but it's not Courtney's fault. She didn't realize…"

"How much you still miss Ross," Liam finished. "But it must have been hard, watching the video. You and Ross were high school sweethearts, and you thought you'd be together for the rest of your lives. To lose him like that…"

Anna closed her eyes.

Was it wrong that she grieved the loss of the handsome, charismatic boy she'd known in high school more than she grieved the husband who'd taken his frustration out on her when life didn't go the way he'd expected it would?

Anna wanted to start over. Maybe the best way to do that was with the truth.

"I lost Ross way before the car accident," Anna whispered.

Liam stilled beside her. "What do you mean?"

"You…you were right about him, Liam."

It took a moment for the words to sink in, and, even then, Liam wanted to reject them.

"Are you saying that Ross—" Bile rose in Liam's throat, making it difficult to say the word. "Hit you?"

Anna nodded and tucked her knees closer to her heart in a small but telling gesture that just about wrecked him.

"Ross changed after we got married. Or maybe he didn't. Maybe I just didn't see the warning signs like you did." Anna released a shuddering breath. "He could be so charming and sweet…"

"As long as things went his way," Liam finished softly.

He'd witnessed his dad push his mom around and belittle her until she'd started to believe she was all the things Darren claimed she was. A bad mother. A lazy wife. Liam wasn't surprised she'd become withdrawn and turned to alcohol to numb the pain.

"And if something didn't go right, he either blamed me or expected me to fix it."

Prom night.

Liam hadn't realized he'd said the words out loud until Anna nodded.

"I was supposed to make dinner reservations for us that night. None of our friends could afford to go to Twin Pines, but Ross didn't care. He wanted to go there because it was the best.

"The hostess checked the reservation list, and our names weren't on it. Ross tried to charm her into giving us a table, but there was a golf tournament that day and they were booked solid. We ended up having a hamburgers at a little drive-in, instead. Ross was upset... He said I should have called and confirmed the reservation. But I was on the decorating committee and I got so busy I forgot. I apologized, but Ross refused to talk to me during dinner or on the way back to town."

Because Ross would have had to admit to his friends the expensive steak dinner he'd been bragging about all week had fallen through.

Liam had heard Ross brag about a lot of things in the locker room before PE. He'd bragged about his football stats and how he was going to make the pros and have enough money to buy the town someday. Liam hadn't cared about any of that. What had made him sick was when Ross talked about Anna as if she were one of his trophies.

"When I saw Ross grab your arm...I'm guessing that's when he decided to talk?"

Anna nodded. "I was in a hurry to show off my new dress."

Liam still remembered Anna's dress. All

her friends had worn pastel colors, but the one Anna had chosen matched the golden flecks in her eyes. Every time she'd moved, the sequins sewn onto the fabric had sparkled like dew on the grass. She'd looked like princess in a fairy tale.

Sunni was the one who'd talked Liam into going to prom, but he'd taken one lap around the gymnasium and felt as out of place as a canoe in a parking lot. He'd been on his way to his car when Anna and Ross arrived.

"Ross had a temper, but it was the first time he'd laid a hand on me like that. I told myself he didn't realize he'd hurt my arm, but when you told me your mom had made excuses for your dad, it touched a nerve," Anna admitted. "I didn't *want* you to be right. And then Ross came outside and saw us together, and I was afraid—"

"I wouldn't have let him touch you again."

"I was afraid for *you*," Anna said. "I knew Ross had a grudge against your family because of Les Atkins, and I didn't want to give him a reason to act on it."

The admission blew Liam away.

Anna looked up at him. "I'm sorry I said those things to you, Liam. I knew they weren't true and I felt awful. I even told Ross I planned to apologize to you the next day."

"I'm sure he expressed his opinion about that."

"He suggested I stay away from you because you…had a crush on me, and he didn't trust you."

Apparently, Liam hadn't hidden his feelings for Anna as well as he'd thought.

"Ross had suggested we elope, but I always thought he was teasing. After prom night, he started to bring it up more often. Ross had all these reasons why we should get married right away, and I was flattered he didn't want to wait a few years. He said we belonged together."

Anna belongs to me, Kane.

With Ross, it was all about winning.

Eddie's words flashed through Liam's mind.

Ross was afraid Anna would break up with him and go out with you.

Liam assumed it was the beer talking, but was it possible Ross had seen *him* as competition?

The idea would have made Liam laugh…if he wasn't sick to his stomach at the thought of what Anna might have gone through after Ross slipped a ring on her finger.

A part of him didn't want to go there, but he wasn't going to let Anna walk through the shadows of those memories alone.

"What did you mean when you said things got worse after you and Ross eloped?"

He felt the shiver that rocketed through Anna and he folded his hand over hers, which was icy cold in spite of the balmy temperature. She was

silent for so long Liam wasn't sure he would find
out the rest of the story.

He wasn't sure he *wanted* to know.

*God, remind Anna how much You love her.
Heal her heart. It doesn't matter if she trusts
me...but I pray she trusts You with this burden.
She's been carrying it too long.*

"We'd decided that I would work until Ross
graduated from college and then it would be my
turn to get a degree," Anna finally said. "I found
a job waitressing and Ross started football practice.

"He was used to being the star on the football
team and he felt a lot of pressure to prove himself all over again. When Ross wasn't at practice
he was hanging out with his teammates. If I suggested we spend some time together, he accused
me of not supporting his dreams."

Liam struggled to control his rising anger.
From what Anna had just told him, she'd done
nothing *but* support the guy.

"When I found out I was pregnant the next
year, Ross accused me of trying to manipulate
him into staying home more. The twins were
born premature, and I quit my job to stay home
and take care of them. Ross began to spend more
and time away from us because he said the stress
at home made it hard to concentrate on the field."

And when he was home, he'd taken his stress out on Anna.

Liam couldn't imagine how alone and isolated Anna had felt when the person who'd promised to love and cherish her through the good and the bad had all but abandoned her when she'd needed him the most.

"His grades started to slip and he got a letter from the dean that his scholarship was in danger. It started to affect his playing, too. The coach told Ross that if he didn't shape up, the recruiters wouldn't take a chance on him. But instead of shaping up, he started drinking with some guys he'd met in class."

"Anna." Her name tumbled out on a groan. "Didn't you tell your mom what was going on? Or Ross's parents?"

"He made me promise I wouldn't tell anyone. Ross said that asking for help was weak...that his dad had raised him to stand on his own two feet. I knew Douglas could be critical and overbearing at times, but I never thought Ross would turn out to be like him." Anna averted her gaze. "I wanted to tell Mom, but my pride got in the way, too. It was hard to admit I was...failing as a wife."

"Ross failed *you*, Anna, when he didn't keep his vows. You and the twins were his priority, not his football career."

"The n-night Ross died, he was upset because he'd heard rumors that the coach was going to replace him. I tried to convince him to stay home but he pushed me out of the way. On the way home…his car went off the road. His blood alcohol level was within the legal limit but he took a corner too fast and lost control."

Liam closed his eyes. Another burden she'd carried alone.

When the news had broken about Ross's accident, the local newspaper had focused on his accomplishments, not the details surrounding the accident. Liam had seen a photograph of Anna accepting a plaque from Emerson's athletic club in his memory after she returned to Castle Falls.

"You can't blame yourself. Nothing you could have said or done would have stopped Ross from leaving that night."

Hearing Liam say the words out loud lifted the weight of another burden Anna had carried for years.

She'd replayed the scene over and over in her mind, wishing she had done things differently. She was Ross's wife—she should have known he would go out drinking with his friends. Should have been brave enough to grab his car keys so he couldn't leave.

All the "should haves" that had added to her guilt.

"You followed your instincts," Liam said softly. "If you'd tried to stop Ross from leaving, you and the twins might have been the ones in danger."

The quiet statement blew her away.

"How did you know that?" Anna whispered.

"Because I lived it," he said simply.

The one person who understood what Anna had gone through was the one she'd kept her distance from for years. And maybe Liam wouldn't have felt so alone, either.

Liam shifted beside her. "Anna—"

"Anna!" Courtney's voice drifted through the trees.

"Everyone is leaving for the fireworks."

Liam caught Anna's hand as she started to rise. "I'll tell her to go ahead without you."

"I can't." Anna attempted a smile. "Class president, remember?"

Anna was paraphrasing words he'd said the day of the canoe trip, but Liam didn't smile back. He folded her in his arms and pressed a kiss against her hair.

"Thank you," he murmured in her ear. "For trusting me."

"Trust… It isn't easy for me," Anna admitted.

But she was ready to let God help her with that, too.

Chapter Nineteen

"Are you sure you don't want to ride along with me to Timber Shores today?" Aiden secured the last canoe on the trailer. "Show off your brand-new babies?"

"Not this time." Liam nudged his brother aside and checked the tie-down on the back of the pickup. "I already have plans."

"That's right." Aiden slapped Liam on the back. "It's Wednesday. You're going to chaperone the Sunflowers and show off your outdoor skills, instead. I think I'd rather dive off the top of Miner's Castle than go on a scavenger hunt with a group of third-grade girls."

"Coward."

"You're calling *me* a coward?" Aiden's eyebrows shot up into his hairline. "The guy who still hasn't asked a certain redhead out for dinner?"

"I'm waiting for the right time."

"Uh-huh. And that would be…"

"Tonight, okay? The Sunflowers are making root-beer floats for all the parents when we get back from the scavenger hunt."

Liam hadn't talked to Anna since Saturday night. He'd looked for her at the fireworks, but Courtney said she'd left early. At church the next morning, he'd figured out why. Both Nancy Foster and Anna's grandmother were sitting between Anna and the twins when he'd arrived.

An army of elderly women had surrounded them after the service—Liam's own mother being one of them—so it hadn't been exactly the best time to approach Anna and ask her on a date.

Hosting the reunion had put Liam behind in other areas, so he'd spent Monday and Tuesday in the workshop playing catch-up. It had also given him time to sort through the things Anna had told him about Ross. He'd prayed through the tangle of emotions, laying everything—anger, regret, grief—at God's feet until there was one thing left.

Hope.

Liam didn't want to let go of that. No matter how difficult it must have been for Anna to confide in him, he wanted to believe it meant she was finally ready to step out from the shadows of the past.

"That isn't the most romantic setting," Aiden's voice broke into his thoughts. "But you'll get the hang of it eventually."

Liam rolled his eyes. "Thanks."

"Anytime. Practice makes perfect." Aiden grinned. "And can I help it that I've had a lot of practice?"

Practice asking a girl out on a first date, maybe, but as far as Liam knew, his baby brother had never followed up with a second or a third.

Still, he was relieved Aiden was in a frame of mind to tease him again. After Brendan had broken the news about their sister, Aiden had become increasingly distant, spending more time on the river than with the family. It was good to see him acting more like himself.

Liam gave one of the canoes he'd finished an affectionate pat. "Take care of them."

Aiden wasn't paying any attention to him. He was watching a vehicle turn the corner of the driveway. "Give me your best guess? Insurance salesman or midlife crisis?"

Liam's breath backed up in his lungs when he recognized Douglas Leighton's black Mercedes.

"Trouble," he muttered. "You can finish getting ready. I'll talk to him."

"Okay by me. Lily baked an apple pie this morning, and if I don't claim a piece now, it will be gone before I get back tonight."

Aiden veered toward the house, leaving Liam alone to face Ross's father.

"Mr. Leighton." Liam tried to ignore the knot that formed in his gut as the man got out of the car. "Is there something I can do for you?"

"For me?" The sneer on Douglas's face was identical to the one Liam had seen so often on Ross's face. When no one else was around, of course. "I'm here to do something for you."

"And what would that be?"

"Save you from the embarrassment of showing up at the church and finding out that I'll be the one accompanying my granddaughters on their outing this afternoon."

A curious numbness began to flow through Liam when he should have been shocked by Douglas's announcement.

Why wasn't he shocked?

Because you were afraid this would happen.

Liam shut down the mocking voice. "Why didn't Anna tell me about the change in plans herself?"

"She was afraid you'd be upset and she wanted to avoid a potentially awkward situation," Douglas said. "Castle Falls is a small town. It's easy for people to get the wrong idea…"

Like you did.

The unspoken words settled on Liam's chest like an anchor.

Because they were true.

It's hard for me to trust, Anna had said.

She hadn't been confiding in Liam. She'd been *warning* him.

Liam forced himself to look Douglas in the eye. "Tell Anna I understand."

And, after what she'd gone through with Ross, he couldn't blame her for not trusting him, either.

"A new design?"

Anna's mom peeked over her shoulder and watched Anna thread a glass bead onto a thin piece of dyed hemp. "I love the shade of blue you chose. It reminds me of the color of the river when the sun is coming up."

Anna ducked her head to hide the blush she felt coming on. Because the color reminded *her* of Liam's eyes.

"It's going to be part of the Legacy collection Lily wants to sell when they open the trading post this fall." Anna had stayed up late the past several nights, filling her sketchbook with ideas. "She and Brendan are going to start offering special weekend packages to encourage families and couples to come back every year. They want Castle Falls Outfitters to be a tradition, not just a business."

Lily had pulled her aside after church on Sunday and shared Rich Mason's vision, but Anna had a feeling she knew who'd been instrumental in inviting her to be part of it.

Nancy picked up a tiny silver charm. "An otter?"

"Ben…or Jerry." Anna smiled at the memory. "I've never created a special line for children, but I ran the idea past my two toughest critics and they loved the idea of adding charms to remember things they saw along the way."

"I'm so proud of you, sweetheart." Nancy squeezed Anna's shoulder. "A lot of people have a gift, but not everyone finds the courage to pursue it. Every time I come up here, I'm amazed at what you've accomplished." She chuckled. "Gram tells everyone about your website, you know. And she models your jewelry whenever we go out. Don't be surprised if she starts asking for a commission."

"Really?" Anna bit her lip. "I wasn't sure Gram approved of the idea. You talked about converting the second floor into another dining area for years."

"This is a much better use of the space," Nancy said firmly.

The words warmed Anna's heart.

"My biggest challenge is finding the time…" She glanced at the clock and groaned. "I'm sorry, Mom. I had no idea it was getting so late. Rene wants the parents to pick up the girls at the church and they'll be back from the scavenger hunt in half an hour."

Nancy put her hand on Anna's arm. "Hold

on a minute, sweetheart. There's something I wanted to dis—"

"There you are!" Gram's lilting voice preceded her entrance into the studio. "Marty Jensen called a few minutes ago and he wants us to have a booth at the fall festival in September. We'll make a batch of cinnamon ice cream and serve it over a slice of homemade apple pie. Maybe I'll even experiment a little and see if I can do something with pumpkin…"

"Hold on a second, Gram." Anna reached for her cell phone. "I have to check my calendar and make sure I'm free that weekend. It will be football season, so it's difficult to coax the teenagers who worked for me all summer to give up a weekend, especially if there's something going on in town."

Gram frowned at Anna's mother. "You haven't told her yet?"

Nancy rolled her eyes at the ceiling. "You didn't give me a chance, Mom."

"Told me what?" Anna set down the phone and swiveled the stool so she faced the two women. "What's going on?"

"I'm not going back to Florida," Gram announced.

"Not going back… But I thought you loved Florida."

"I love my family more," Gram said. "And the

last time I looked, they were all living right here in Castle Falls."

Anna glanced at her mom to gauge how she was taking Gram's abrupt change of heart. To her relief, Nancy was nodding in approval.

"We didn't say anything right away because Gram wanted to pray about it first." Her mom's eyes sparkled. "We didn't realize God would answer so quickly."

"He has to when you're my age," Gram retorted. "I told the Lord I wanted to do more than spend my days sitting by the pool and beating everyone at pickle ball. He blessed me with good health, and I decided to put it to good use right here."

Here meaning Castle Falls or…

Anna swallowed hard.

"You want to work for me?" she asked cautiously.

"Work for you?" Gram's eyebrows disappeared into the puff of silver hair on her forehead. "Of course not! Tell her, Nancy."

Anna's mom shot Gram an exasperated look. "Gram and I had a little talk last night. You're so busy with the twins, and you sneak up here to your studio every chance you get—"

"But don't worry. You can still fill in behind the counter once in a while," Gram cut in. "And you can keep your studio. If we decide to expand down the road, we'll knock out the wall and join forces with Olivia's coffee shop."

Keep her studio...*knock out a wall*?

"Wait a minute..." Anna pressed her hand against the back of her neck to ward off the headache she felt coming on. "I'm not sure I understand what this means."

"It means," Gram said cheerfully, "you're fired."

Fired.

Anna drove to the church on autopilot.

Laughter bubbled up inside and she finally gave in and let it have its way.

Anna wasn't the only one who'd been excited about the change in management. Her grandmother was practically glowing when she'd shooed Anna out the door of The Happy Cow.

It hadn't occurred to her that Gram was lonely living so far away from family and friends.

Anna couldn't wait to tell the twins that both their grandmas would be living with them again. And she couldn't wait to tell Liam she would have a little more free time.

And if that wasn't a big enough hint that Anna wanted to spend that free time with him, she might have to enlist Sunni's help.

The sun was already setting when Anna turned into the church parking lot. There was no sign of the twins, but Pastor Seth was unloading backpacks from the van. From his sunburned cheeks and bedraggled appearance, it looked as if he'd just finished one of those extreme obstacle courses instead of chaperoning a scavenger hunt with a group of little girls.

Anna jogged over to him. "How did it go?"

"You want to know which team won, don't you?"

"I shouldn't." Anna bit her lip. "But since you brought it up…"

Seth laughed. "Team Leighton finished first," he said.

"Rene made Hannah an honorary Sunflower for the day. She helped decorate the float for the parade last weekend so Cassie made sure she got one of the special pins you made, too."

Hannah, Seth and Rebecca's adorable three-year-old daughter, "helped" with most of the activities at the church.

Anna pictured Liam sporting the bright yellow flower on his collar and smiled. "I hope you got a picture of Liam wearing his pin."

"Liam?" Confusion clouded Seth's eyes. "He didn't go on the scavenger hunt with us."

It took a moment for the pastor's words to sink in. "What do you mean he didn't go with you? Did something happen? Is he okay?" The questions running through Anna's mind barely kept pace with her rising panic.

Liam wouldn't break a promise to the twins without a good reason. And if he had a good reason, he would have called to let her know. *Someone* would have let her know. Sunni. Lily…

"I'm sure Liam is fine," Seth said. "When Douglas got here, all he said was that he was taking Liam's place."

"Douglas?" Anna echoed.

Some of Anna's panic must have shown in her eyes, because Seth's confusion changed to concern. "I'm sorry, Anna. I assumed your father-in-law had your permission to accompany the girls today."

Anna swallowed the lump forming in her throat.

Douglas wouldn't have…

Yes. He would. She should have known her former father-in-law would take matters into his own hands after he'd seen her and Liam together on Saturday.

"Is Douglas still here?"

"No, he left a few minutes ago." Seth reached out and gave Anna's arm a bracing squeeze. "Rene and the girls are in the kitchen making root-beer floats and I heard her tell one of the parents they'd be here at least another hour. If you'd like, Rebecca and I can keep an eye on the twins until you get back."

Anna choked out her thanks and sprinted

across the parking lot to her van. She gripped the steering wheel to stop her hands from shaking, but it didn't calm the emotions roiling inside.

The fifteen-minute drive to Douglas and Barbara's house seemed to take forever. The lights were still on when she pulled up in front of the door.

Douglas opened it before Anna had a chance to ring the bell.

"I saw your van." Surprise flickered in Douglas's eyes. "What are you doing here, Anna?"

She couldn't believe he had to ask. "Do you mind if I come in for a minute, Douglas?"

"Are the girls with you?" His gaze shifted to her vehicle.

"No, they're with Seth and Rebecca Tamblin."

"Douglas, who on earth—" Barbara emerged from a doorway farther down the hall and froze when she spotted Anna. "Is everything all right?"

Anna dragged in a shaky breath. "Actually… everything isn't all right, Barbara. I would like to talk to Douglas about the scavenger hunt."

"I don't know why it couldn't wait until tomorrow, but you don't have to discuss it in the foyer." Ross's mother motioned toward the living room. "Come in and sit down."

Anna followed the couple, but she was too restless to sit.

"Douglas said the twins won the competition

today." Barbara locked her fingers together at her waist, a nervous gesture Anna had seen before.

"Of course they won," Douglas growled. "They're Leightons, aren't they?"

Douglas hadn't gone with the Sunflowers because he wanted to spend time with his granddaughters. In fact, Anna doubted it had anything to do with Cassie and Chloe at all. He hadn't taken Liam's place as much he'd wanted to *put* Liam in his place.

"What did you say to Liam?" Anna struggled to keep her tone even. "He took an afternoon off from work so he could go with the twins today."

"If Cassie and Chloe are going to spend time with someone, it should be family," Douglas snapped, proving Anna's theory had been correct.

She gripped the back of the chair and sent up a silent prayer for strength. "I'm their mother," Anna reminded him. "You should have discussed it with me first."

"I would have, but I'm not sure I trust your judgment anymore, Anna." Blotches of color broke out on Douglas's face. "Not when *you* trust a man like Liam Kane with my granddaughters."

"Liam has been nothing but kind to Cassie and Chloe over the past few weeks." He'd been kind to her, too. Even when Anna had done her best to push him away.

"Kind," Douglas scoffed. "I didn't want to tell you this because it stretches the boundaries of attorney-client privilege, but you need to know the kind of man you've been allowing my granddaughters to spend time with." Anger kindled in Douglas's eyes. "When Sunni insisted on going forward with the adoption, she contacted my law firm. My partner drew up the paperwork, and he asked me to make sure everything was in order.

"The social worker included the Kane family history and what I saw in their background was troubling. They came from an extremely dysfunctional home, and even the caseworker expressed reservations about placing them with the Masons."

"You can't hold Liam responsible for the things his parents did," Anna said. "He was a child. Liam has lived in Castle Falls for years, and he's never been in trouble."

"He was never *arrested*," Douglas corrected her. "But only because Ross convinced me not to press charges."

"Ross?" The floor tilted underneath Anna's feet.

"My son never told you that Liam started a fight with him one night? He came at Ross with no provocation…other than the fact he was jealous of him."

"I don't believe that."

"Ask Barbara." Anger ignited in Douglas's eyes. "She was there when Ross came home."

Anna's stomach churned when Barbara nodded in affirmation.

"We had to pay for Ross's tuxedo jacket because there were bloodstains on it."

"Tuxedo?"

"It happened the night of your senior prom."

Anna's stomach churned as she tried to digest that information. Ross had been angry at Liam for interfering, but they'd exchanged words, not punches. She and Ross had gone back inside the gymnasium…and then he'd dropped Anna off at home a half hour before her curfew. She remembered thinking that was strange at the time, but she hadn't questioned him about it.

Liam hadn't said a word about Ross picking a fight with him because he wanted to protect her from more pain. Anna knew it to be true—just like she knew the blood on Ross's hands—and shirt—wasn't his. Liam had seen too much violence when he was growing up. He wouldn't have fought back.

"I'm not going to hold Liam's past against him," Anna said.

Douglas looked at her in disgust. "Kane isn't going to change."

Anna smiled, her heart curiously light.

"I wouldn't want him to."

Chapter Twenty

Shadows stretched across the yard, as dark as the windows of Liam's workshop. Anna hadn't expected him to be working this late at night, but there were no lights glowing in the apartment above the garage, either.

Was he working at the cabin?

"Anna? Is that you?"

Anna whirled toward Lily with a cry of relief. "I have to talk to Liam. Do you know where he is?"

"I haven't seen him since this morning." Her friend wore an oversize sweatshirt and leggings, evidence she'd already settled in for the evening, but she stepped off the porch and danced her way, barefoot, across the dew-soaked grass until she reached Anna's side. "Come inside for a few minutes, before the mosquitoes carry you away."

Anna allowed Lily to take her by the elbow

and steer her toward the log home Brendan had moved into before the couple got married.

"Hey, Anna." Brendan was sprawled on the couch, a bowl of popcorn the size of a wash-tub on the coffee table in front of him. "How's it going?"

Anna decided that a simple question deserved a simple answer.

"Terrible."

Lily gasped, but Brendan didn't look the least bit surprised by Anna's response.

"There seems to be a lot of that going around," he murmured.

Lily gave Anna a sidelong glance but didn't waste time asking her husband to explain himself. "Anna wants to talk to Liam. Is he working on the cabin?"

Brendan shook his head. "Aiden had to deliver some canoes to Timber Shores today, and Liam decided to ride along with him."

Clearly this was news to Lily. "When will they be home?"

"I'm not sure. It's a long trip, and they got a late start—" Brendan glanced at Anna. "If Mae decided Aiden was too tired to make the drive back, she'll order him to bunk with her guides for the night and get a fresh start in the morning."

Anna tried to hide her discouragement, but

when Lily slipped an arm through hers, she realized she hadn't done a very good job.

"Did you try to call him?" Lily asked.

"Yes." Four times. And every time, the call had gone straight to Liam's voice mail. "He isn't answering his phone."

"Aiden has mentioned there are a lot of dead zones up there," Brendan said. "They might have given up and turned their phones off."

Or Liam didn't want to talk to her.

What reason had Douglas given Liam for taking his place?

"Thanks…" Anna swallowed around the lump in her throat. "I should go… Rebecca is keeping an eye on the twins for me."

Lily followed her outside.

"Whatever happened between you and Liam… you'll work it out, Anna." A smile tipped her lips. "I'm not an expert on relationships, but it's obvious that he has feelings for you."

Anna couldn't quite muster a smile.

Because, right now, the most important thing to Anna was telling Liam how she felt about *him*.

"Are you sure I can't offer you a job, Aiden?"

Mae Lawrence, the director of Timber Shores Retreat Center, tossed her hat onto the table and slid along the bench across from Liam and Aiden.

"I've got a dozen college students coming here

for leadership training tomorrow, and one of my adventure guides canceled out on me because of family issues."

Aiden moved Mae's camouflage ball cap—an item of clothing the counselors teasingly referred to as their boss's favorite "fashion" accessory—away from a puddle of maple syrup.

It was Liam's first time visiting the retreat center, but Aiden had driven back and forth several times, delivering canoes or training a group of new counselors. His last trip had been the weekend of the animal-shelter benefit, when Liam had been drafted to take his place as the mascot.

And danced with Anna…

He wasn't going to think about Anna.

"It's tempting." Aiden snagged a piece of bacon off Liam's plate. "But then *I* would be the one with family issues if I bailed in the middle of the tourist season."

"Even if I told you the college students are all members of a sorority?"

"Nope." There was a heartbeat of silence. "Are they?"

Mae laughed. "You and I both know it wouldn't make a difference. But, like my daddy always said, it never hurts to ask."

"I'll do it," Liam said.

Liam wasn't sure who looked more shocked by the announcement—his brother or Mae.

Aiden's fork clattered against his plate. "Liam…"

"I'm caught up on our orders, and Mae needs the help." Liam shot the director a questioning glance to confirm her offer had been sincere.

She grinned. "Oh, Mae *definitely* needs the help. You can bunk with the other guides at the lodge, and I'll even let you snag an extra set of clothes from the general store. Our logo is on everything from T-shirts to tube socks."

"You're forgetting something," Aiden said. "If you stay here, how am I supposed to get home?"

"You could hitchhike." Mischief danced in Mae's eyes. "Or you could borrow my Harley."

Aiden opened his mouth. Closed it again.

"Great." Liam wadded up his napkin and tossed it on his plate, covering the scrambled eggs he'd barely touched. "Then it's settled."

Aiden's expression warned Liam the matter was far from settled, but at least he waited until they were outside the cafeteria—and out of Mae's earshot—before he made his opinion known.

"You're really not coming home with me?"

"It's only a few days." And, at the moment, home was the last place Liam wanted to be.

"Fine," Aiden muttered. "But I'm holding you to that."

"Worried you'll have to build the canoes?"

For once, Aiden didn't crack a joke in return. "Worried about my big brother."

Liam's throat suddenly felt scratchy. "I'm good."

"Uh-huh." Aiden didn't look convinced. "What am I supposed to tell Mom?"

"That I'll back on Saturday."

"You better be." Aiden thumped him on the back. "Or I'll tell her you decided to keep all those kittens—and the mama, too."

With that threat hanging over Liam's head, his brother sauntered toward the pickup truck.

After Aiden left, Liam wasn't quite ready to socialize with the other guides. Timber Shores Retreat Center had been built on the site of an old logging camp, and, although it had undergone a major expansion after Mae took over as director, a two-million-dollar makeover hadn't stripped the grounds of its original charm.

Liam followed the worn footpath around the lake and ended up at an old fishing pier. Hemmed in by cattails, the boards had weathered to pale silver, and one of them shifted underneath Liam's feet as he walked to the end and sat down.

It would have been better if things had stayed the way they were between Anna and me, God.

He wouldn't know what he was missing.

Wouldn't have fallen in love with her.

How could he create new memories with Anna when the old ones kept getting in the way?

When she'd changed her mind at the last minute and asked Douglas Leighton to take his place, he'd realized she didn't really trust him. Leaving him in charge of her business wasn't on the same level as entrusting her daughters to his care.

Liam felt the ache of what Anna had gone through like a physical pain.

Would she ever be able to trust a man after what she'd gone through?

No matter how hard Liam tried to ignore it, one of the things Anna had said kept cycling through his mind.

I didn't think Ross would turn out like his father.

And there it was. The reason Anna couldn't completely trust him. What if Liam turned out to be like his father, too?

I didn't want to be right about Ross, Lord, but I want her to find freedom in knowing how much You love her. It's more important that she trusts You.

The sheet of gray clouds matched Anna's mood as she looked out the window of her studio on Saturday afternoon. It had been two days since Lily had called and broken the news that Aiden had returned home alone. The retreat center was short a guide, so Liam had volunteered to stay for a few days to help out.

Liam. The man who preferred to work in his shop.

Anna had thought about leaving another voice mail, but she wasn't sure Liam would be checking his phone. And, even if he did, Anna wouldn't be able to condense everything she wanted to say in a short message. She needed to see Liam's face when she told him that Douglas hadn't had her permission to take the twins on the scavenger hunt.

But what if he didn't return her call? Should she show up at his front door? Sit next to him in the church tomorrow morning?

She guided a charm onto a piece of wire and gave it a twist. Now that Anna's mother and Gram had taken over The Happy Cow, Anna had plenty of time to work on the Legacy line. By the time the trading post was in operation, Liam would need more shelves to display the new jewelry.

The ice-cream shop was closed for the day, so Anna had taken advantage of the quiet to spend a few hours in her studio. But suddenly she realized it was *too* quiet.

She slid off the stool and walked to the doorway. Cassie and Chloe had skipped into her office to work on their next Sunflower activity the moment she'd unlocked the door of The Happy Cow. Anna had heard them chattering, giggling and even singing the club's theme song, but she didn't hear so much as a peep from them now. And they hadn't napped since they were two years old.

"Girls?"

Silence.

The river was strictly off-limits, but Anna had a heart-stopping vision of the twins slipping outside and going down there to play. She took the stairs two at a time and bolted toward the back door.

A flash of pink caught Anna's eye as she passed the office and relief turned her knees to liquid.

"Hi, Mom."

The girls looked up as Anna staggered into the room.

Magic Markers littered the braided rug, and both her daughters were sprawled on their stomachs, coloring on a gigantic piece of poster board.

"Now I know why you've been so quiet," Anna teased. "What are you working on?"

"Something for Liam." Cassie rolled to her knees. "Do you think he'll like it? He can hang it on the door—"

"And now he won't have to make one."

The girls scooted backward so Anna could

take a closer look. And what she saw was a gigantic, lopsided canoe. Not in the traditional colors of red or yellow, either. Cassie and Chloe had glued strips of brown construction paper to the poster board, carefully and painstakingly crafting it to resemble one of the vintage designs Liam preferred. A shiny gold tree with spreading branches—the Castle Falls logo—graced the bow.

"You did a wonderful job, but I thought you were working on your next pin."

"We are." Chloe grinned. "But this time, Ms. Shapiro said we could pick out any one on the list that we wanted to, so Chloe and I picked this one—"

"Surprise someone you love," Chloe finished. "Do you think it's a good idea, Mom?"

"I think…" Anna blinked back the tears that welled up in her eyes. "It's a very good idea."

Chapter Twenty-One

Liam had pulled out slivers, gone through every bandage in the first-aid kit and dived into the water to rescue a backpack before it sank to the bottom of the river.

And that was *before* they launched the canoes.

Still, he would have stayed at the retreat center another day or two—or week—if Mae had asked. Liam respected Anna's decision, but that didn't mean it would be easy to see her at New Life Fellowship on Sunday mornings or on his occasional forays into town.

The trailer rattled as Liam turned onto the bridge.

The Saturday before, Anna had fastened balloon bouquets to the railing so their classmates wouldn't miss the turn on their way to the reunion. A week that seemed like a lifetime ago now.

Liam pulled up in front of the garage, and

the first thing he noticed were the empty spaces where his family's vehicles were usually parked.

Thank You, Lord.

He'd texted Sunni from the gas station when he'd left Timber Shores, but he wasn't quite ready to face his family yet. If Aiden had sensed something was wrong, Liam was afraid he'd be the guest of honor at another family meeting.

He hopped out of the cab and unhooked the trailer, trying not to look at the grove of trees where his last conversation with Anna had taken place. After tent camping for three days, he needed a hot shower, food and clothing that wasn't covered with smiley-faced pine trees.

But first he had to check on Feathers and her kittens.

Dodging puddles and fallen leaves, he made his way to the workshop. Another place that reminded him of Anna.

Oh, who was he kidding? Everything reminded him of Anna.

He flipped on the light and walked inside, but the cardboard box was empty. No sign of his furry welcoming committee.

Liam's gaze traveled over the shelves—one of the kittens' favorite places to nap—and snagged on the door between his workshop and the storage room.

How had he *not* noticed the door.

The top half was covered with a large canoe-shaped sign, with Trading Post spelled out in gold glitter from bow to stern. Given the fact Liam's brothers weren't exactly gold-glitter kind of guys, Liam had a pretty good idea who had put it there.

The ache that had taken up residence in his chest tripled in size.

This was going to kill him. This was—

"Surprise!"

The door swung open, and Cassie and Chloe jumped out in front of him.

Anna *knew* the first thing Liam would do when he got home was check on Feathers and her kittens.

His hair was mussed and a three-day growth of beard shadowed his jaw, but, to Anna, he'd never looked more appealing.

Because he was *here*.

The speech Anna had rehearsed dissolved when their eyes met over the twins' heads.

"Hi," she said simply.

God bless Cassie and Chloe. They did what Anna was too afraid to do—charged toward Liam and threw themselves into his arms.

"Do you like the sign we made—"

"We used a *whole* bottle of glue."

Liam smiled. "It's great. No, better than great. It's awesome."

The girls beamed.

"Lily told us when you'd be home and we wanted to surprise you," Chloe told him.

"Our legs got tired." Cassie rubbed her bare knees. "Because you're kind of late."

The perfect segue, Anna decided.

"Girls…why don't you take the kittens outside for a few minutes," she suggested. "I'm sure they would like to stretch their legs, too."

"Okay!" Liam got another hug before the twins scooped up the kittens and disappeared out the door.

Anna got the feeling Liam would have followed if she hadn't stepped in front of him.

"Liam…can I talk to you a minute?"

"Sure." He speared his hands into the front pockets of his jeans, a casual gesture at complete odds with the guarded look in his eyes.

Physically, he was only a few feet away, but Anna felt the distance between them widen.

Help me, Lord.

She sent up a silent prayer, not knowing how— or even where—to begin.

"I'm sorry." When in doubt, Anna had learned that was a good place to start. "I didn't know

Douglas had gone on the scavenger hunt until I went to the church to pick up the girls last Wednesday."

Liam's expression didn't change. "It doesn't matter."

It wasn't what Anna had expected him to say. Because it *did* matter. And she refused to let him build a wall between them again.

"What do you mean it doesn't matter?" Anna protested. "Douglas led you to believe that he had my permission to take your place."

"It doesn't matter because you'll always have doubts about me. I can't change my past or my family history. And now that I know what Ross did…how can I blame you for not trusting me?"

"It was never about trusting you," Anna said. "I didn't trust myself. I was afraid to get close to you because I didn't want to make another mistake. But I know I would be making a bigger one if I didn't tell you the truth."

A muscle worked in Liam's jaw. "That you aren't ready to fall in love again?"

"No," Anna whispered. "That I already have."

Liam stared at her as if he couldn't believe those words had just come out of her mouth.

"I love you, Liam, and—" Anna gasped as Liam closed the distance between them and pulled her into his arms. Kissed her with a heady blend of passion and tenderness until Anna couldn't imagine a future without Liam. Without this.

"I love you, too," he murmured against her lips.

Over the pounding of her heart, she heard the faint creak of the door. Followed by a giggle.

"They're *kissing*."

"Does that mean they're going to get married?"

Anna felt Liam's smile against her lips before he released her.

Cassie and Chloe stood just inside the door, hands over their mouths, eyes wide with shocked delight.

"Girls…" Anna felt her cheeks ignite. "It's a little early for questions like that."

Cassie tipped her head. "Why? Because Liam hasn't asked you out for dinner yet?"

"Or bought you flowers?"

"Um…" Anna glanced at Liam. Just as she suspected. He was grinning, not blushing.

"It seems," Liam said in a low voice. "I've skipped a few critical steps." He looked at the twins. "Who's hungry?"

"We are!"

"Then let's go."

"Liam…you don't have to do this," Anna protested.

"Pizza and my favorite girls." Liam winked at her. "I can't imagine a better first date."

Neither could Anna, but it did get better.

Liam stopped at the Petal Pushers flower shop and bought not one, but three bouquets of daisies on the way.

Epilogue

September

"Go for a walk with me?"

Liam's breath whispered against Anna's ear and triggered a shiver that swept all the way down to her toes.

"We can't waste a sunset like this."

Sunset?

At the moment, Anna was perfectly content to lose herself in Liam's blue eyes.

"You should go, Mom." Cassie dragged a French fry through the pool of ketchup on her plate. "We don't mind. Do we, Chloe?"

"Nope!" Chloe said blithely. "I've seen sunsets before."

All right, then.

"While you're gone, the girls and I will make ice-cream sundaes for dessert," Sunni said, making no attempt whatsoever to hide the fact they'd been eavesdropping.

But then, they *were* sitting at the dinner table with Liam's entire family.

Liam was already on his feet, his hand on the back of Anna's chair.

Another shiver skipped through her—this one anticipation.

Brendan and Lily exchanged a grin.

"Take your time," Lily said.

"Yeah," Aiden called out as Liam guided Anna toward the door. "It's not like ice cream melts or anything."

Brendan cuffed him on the shoulder. "Someday you'll understand, little brother."

Anna heard Aiden's snort of disbelief as she and Liam stepped outside.

"I know a place that has a spectacular view of the sunset," Liam murmured. "If you don't mind walking a little ways."

Anna shook her head. If it meant time with Liam, she would have hiked all the way to the top of Miner's Castle.

Liam wove his fingers through hers as they set out on the path along the river. Anna spotted the stone chimney of Liam's cabin peeking through the trees and felt a pinch of guilt.

"I suppose you haven't had time to work on the cabin very much." Because Liam had been spending the majority of his free time with her and the twins.

"I ran into a little problem."

"What kind of problem?"

Liam shrugged. "It happens sometimes during the building process. You realize something is off."

"If there's anything I can do to help, let me know," Anna offered.

A smile played at the corners of Liam's lips. "Come to think of it, it would be nice to have your opinion on a few things."

"Then we should have brought Cassie and Chloe along. They definitely have an opinion," Anna teased. "'It's a *little* little,'" she said, repeating Chloe's words with a laugh. "We had a discussion on the way home that night about questions you should and shouldn't ask your river guide."

"I don't know." Liam's hand closed around the tiny velvet box in the front pocket of his jeans as they reached the clearing. "Those two little girls are right about a lot of things."

"What kind of problem are you having?" Anna didn't seem to hear him.

"Uh-huh." It was difficult, Liam decided, to talk when the woman you were with took your breath away. "I have to cut down a few more trees."

"It doesn't look like they're in the way."

"They will be." Liam pulled in a breath. Released it again.

"Because that's where your studio is going to be."

"My—" Anna stared at him. "My what?"

"Your studio. I thought you'd want it to face the river." Liam pointed to a towering Norway pine. "And that one needs to go because the spare room has to be big enough for bunk beds and stuffed animals and bookshelves."

Tears welled up in Anna's eyes and she cupped her hands over her mouth, giving Liam the courage to go on.

"I love you, Anna, and I hate going home at night—because home is wherever you and the girls are. You don't just have my heart...you *are* my heart." He pulled the velvet box from his pocket and fumbled with the lid. "It's not as beautiful as the ones you make, of course, but I couldn't exactly commission you to design your own engagement ring…"

Anna stared down in wonder at the solitaire diamond. Set in a band made up of tiny platinum leaves, it was beautiful in its very simplicity.

"It's perfect," she breathed.

"The girls said you'd love it."

"You showed them the ring?"

"Showed them? They helped me pick it out."

"When…"

"Do you remember when Lily took them to the park a few weeks ago?"

"Yes…"

"She handed them over to me when they got there." Liam slipped the ring on her finger. "Will you marry me, Anna?"

"Yes."

More tears.

Liam swept them away with the pad of his thumb. "Brendan didn't warn me that you were going to cry."

"Who else knows you were going to propose to me?" Anna demanded, the gurgle of laughter a counterpoint to the severe look she leveled in his direction.

"Everyone," Liam confessed. "That's what the ice-cream sundaes are for. Standard fare for a Kane celebration, remember?"

Anna's arms locked around Liam's waist, and he closed his eyes. Pressed a kiss against the crown of her head.

Thank You, God, for bringing this woman into my life. For trusting me with her and those two amazing little girls.

"So when can we get married?" he murmured. "Is tomorrow too soon?"

"Tomorrow is a *little* soon." Anna's muffled laugh sent his heart dancing to a crazy rhythm.

But when she peeked up at him through her russet lashes, it almost burst right through his chest.

"Liam?"

"Mmm."

"Now you're supposed to kiss me."

He obliged.

Anna's fingers tangled Liam's hair as he pulled her deeper into the circle of his arms and claimed her lips.

"Soon," she gasped when Liam lifted his head. "Very soon."

The dazed look on her face made him grin. Or maybe it was because he was feeling a little dazed by the power of that kiss, too.

"If we don't go back soon, you know they're going to send out a search party," Liam said.

"And Aiden will complain that his ice cream melted."

"True."

He kissed her again anyway.

By the time they reached Sunni's house, a large crowd had gathered on the patio. Along with Liam's siblings, Anna's mother and grandmother sat next to Sunni at the picnic table. And while they were all smiling, no one made a sound until Anna held up her hand and presented the ring.

The twins squealed and rushed to Anna's side.

"We kept it a secret, Mom!" Cassie's face glowed with pride.

"Can we be your bridesmaids?"

Anna gave him a questioning look—the only detail they'd agreed on between walking and kissing was the wedding date.

"Bridesmaids, it is," Liam said.

"Congratulations, bro." Brendan, whose previous displays of affection or approval usually came in the form of a headlock or fist bump, wrapped his arms around Liam and gave him a hug.

"Have you set a date yet?" Sunni asked.

"I suggested tomorrow." Liam winked at Anna. "But we compromised and decided on Christmas Eve."

Liam couldn't help but notice that Aiden was the only one who didn't look excited by the date they'd picked.

"Aiden?" Anna had picked up on the swift change in his brother's mood, too. "Is something wrong with having the wedding on Christmas Eve?"

"It only gives me four months," Aiden said gruffly.

"Four months to get used to the idea of wearing a tux?" Brendan teased.

Liam grinned. "Four months to find a date?"

Aiden didn't respond in kind. If anything, his expression turned more solemn.

"Four months to find our sister."

Sunni's quiet gasp punctuated the silence, and Anna slipped her hand into Liam's, a silent show of support.

"I would love to meet her," Anna said softly. "Wouldn't you, Liam?"

"Yes." He took advantage of the buzz that broke out after Aiden's announcement to draw her closer. "I love you," he murmured. "You know that, right?"

"I think I'd like to hear it from time to time, just to be sure," Anna whispered back.

"How about a lifetime?"

Anna smiled up at him.

"A lifetime sounds just about right."

It sounded right to Liam, too.

* * * * *

*If you enjoyed THE BACHELOR'S TWINS,
look for the first book in the
CASTLE FALLS series
THE BACHELOR NEXT DOOR.*

Dear Reader,

It was so much fun to return to Castle Falls! When I introduced Cassie and Chloe Leighton in *The Bachelor Next Door*, I didn't realize their mother would be the heroine of my next book. That's the fun of the writing journey!

As a single mom with a secret, Anna placed a heavy burden on herself. I think we can be guilty of that, too, sometimes. We don't want to ask for help because we're afraid people will think we're weak. But guess what? We are! God offers us His strength and He brings people into our lives who will share our burdens.

I hope you enjoyed your visit to Castle Falls! And if you're curious about Aiden's quest for their missing sister, watch for the next book in the series! I love to hear from my readers, so visit my website at www.kathrynspringer.com, and while you're there, be sure to sign up for my free newsletter. It will keep you posted on upcoming releases and special giveaways!

Walk in Joy,

Kathryn Springer

Get 2 Free Books,
Plus 2 Free Gifts —
just for trying the Reader Service!

YES! Please send me 2 FREE Love Inspired® Suspense novels and my 2 FREE mystery gifts (gifts are worth about $10 retail). After receiving them, if I don't wish to receive any more books, I can return the shipping statement marked "cancel." If I don't cancel, I will receive 4 brand-new novels every month and be billed just $5.24 each for the regular-print edition or $5.74 each for the larger-print edition in the U.S., or $5.74 each for the regular-print edition or $6.24 each for the larger-print edition in Canada. That's a savings of at least 13% off the cover price. It's quite a bargain! Shipping and handling is just 50¢ per book in the U.S. and 75¢ per book in Canada.* I understand that accepting the 2 free books and gifts places me under no obligation to buy anything. I can always return a shipment and cancel at any time. Even if I never buy another book, the 2 free books and gifts are mine to keep forever.

Please check one: ☐ Love Inspired Suspense Regular-Print   ☐ Love Inspired Suspense Larger-Print
                            (153/353 IDN GLQE)   (107/307 IDN GLQF)

Name   (PLEASE PRINT)

Address   Apt. #

City   State/Prov.   Zip/Postal Code

Signature (if under 18, a parent or guardian must sign)

Mail to the **Reader Service**:

IN U.S.A.: P.O. Box 1867, Buffalo, NY 14240-1867
IN CANADA: P.O. Box 611, Fort Erie, Ontario L2A 9Z9

Want to try two free books from another series?
Call 1-800-873-8635 or visit www.ReaderService.com.

* Terms and prices subject to change without notice. Prices do not include applicable taxes. Sales tax applicable in N.Y. Canadian residents will be charged applicable taxes. Offer not valid in Quebec. This offer is limited to one order per household. Books received may not be as shown. Not valid for current subscribers to Love Inspired Suspense books. All orders subject to credit approval. Credit or debit balances in a customer's account(s) may be offset by any other outstanding balance owed by or to the customer. Please allow 4 to 6 weeks for delivery. Offer available while quantities last.

Your Privacy—The Reader Service is committed to protecting your privacy. Our Privacy Policy is available online at www.ReaderService.com or upon request from the Reader Service.

We make a portion of our mailing list available to reputable third parties that offer products we believe may interest you. If you prefer that we not exchange your name with third parties, or if you wish to clarify or modify your communication preferences, please visit us at www.ReaderService.com/consumerchoice or write to us at Reader Service Preference Service, P.O. Box 9062, Buffalo, NY 14240-9062. Include your complete name and address.

Get 2 Free Books,
Plus 2 Free Gifts —
just for trying the Reader Service!

♦ HARLEQUIN

HEARTWARMING™

YES! Please send me 2 FREE Harlequin® Heartwarming™ Larger-Print novels and my 2 FREE mystery gifts (gifts worth about $10 retail). After receiving them, if I don't wish to receive any more books, I can return the shipping statement marked "cancel." If I don't cancel, I will receive 4 brand-new larger-print novels every month and be billed just $5.49 per book in the U.S. or $6.24 per book in Canada. That's a savings of at least 19% off the cover price. It's quite a bargain! Shipping and handling is just 50¢ per book in the U.S. and 75¢ per book in Canada.* I understand that accepting the 2 free books and gifts places me under no obligation to buy anything. I can always return a shipment and cancel at any time. Even if I never buy another book, the 2 free books and gifts are mine to keep forever.

161/361 IDN GLQL

Name _____ (PLEASE PRINT) _____

Address _____ Apt. # _____

City _____ State/Prov. _____ Zip/Postal Code _____

Signature (if under 18, a parent or guardian must sign)

Mail to the **Reader Service:**
IN U.S.A.: P.O. Box 1867, Buffalo, NY 14240-1867
IN CANADA: P.O. Box 611, Fort Erie, Ontario L2A 9Z9

Want to try two free books from another line?
Call 1-800-873-8635 today or visit www.ReaderService.com.

* Terms and prices subject to change without notice. Prices do not include applicable taxes. Sales tax applicable in N.Y. Canadian residents will be charged applicable taxes. Offer not valid in Quebec. This offer is limited to one order per household. Books received may not be as shown. Not valid for current subscribers to Harlequin Heartwarming Larger-Print books. All orders subject to credit approval. Credit or debit balances in a customer's account(s) may be offset by any other outstanding balance owed by or to the customer. Please allow 4 to 6 weeks for delivery. Offer available while quantities last.

Your Privacy—The Reader Service is committed to protecting your privacy. Our Privacy Policy is available online at www.ReaderService.com or upon request from the Reader Service.

We make a portion of our mailing list available to reputable third parties that offer products we believe may interest you. If you prefer that we not exchange your name with third parties, or if you wish to clarify or modify your communication preferences, please visit us at www.ReaderService.com/consumerchoice or write to us at Reader Service Preference Service, P.O. Box 9062, Buffalo, NY 14240-9062. Include your complete name and address.